Sending Savannah away had been a simple matter of pragmatism before.

Or that would have been his argument. She was unqualified on all counts, period.

He'd been wrong on one count, the one that mattered most. She was surgically competent. So what excuse could he give GAO—worse, give *her*—as he looked her in the eye and told her to leave? His belief that she would melt in the heat of toil and discomfort was only his opinion. No one, starting with her, was bound to take it.

So what could he say? That he couldn't function with her around? That his mind had emptied of everything but the need to drag her back to his room, rip her out of her clothes and bury himself in her, take her, then take her again until he'd made up for just the first few days of the three years without her?

24/7

The cutting edge of
Mills & Boon® Medical Romance™

The emotion is deep
The drama is real
The passion is fierce

Dear Reader

First chances happen; second chances have to be won. In Savannah Richardson's case, winning a second chance with Javier Sandoval isn't just about working on their relationship and on the fundamental differences between their worlds. It takes her on a quest to uncover her true nature and calling, to overcome her upbringing and to triumph over her weaknesses. Only then can she feel worthy of joining him in the life he's dedicated to humanitarian ambitions.

But Javier also has to make discoveries of his own, to learn among danger and toil and their explosive passion that his iron-clad dedication must give way to the demands of his heart.

Savannah and Javier are two lovers who started out all wrong. When their first relationship ended, it seemed it would be over for ever. Going for the ride with them as they rediscovered each other, and themselves, passed brutal tests and built a unique relationship gave me the greatest satisfaction. I hope their story satisfies you as much.

Olivia Gates

THE DOCTOR'S
LATIN LOVER

BY
OLIVIA GATES

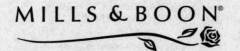

To my husband. You lift me up and you keep me going.

First published in Great Britain 2005
Harlequin Mills & Boon Limited,
Eton House, 18-24 Paradise Road, Richmond, Surrey TW9 1SR

© Olivia Gates 2005

ISBN 0 263 84307 6

Set in Times Roman 10¼ on 11½ pt.
03-0505-52457

Printed and bound in Spain
by Litografia Rosés, S.A., Barcelona

PROLOGUE

THEY were gaining on her.

They were chasing her for more than her purse and jewelry. For more than her body and all the sick, violent freedoms they wanted with it.

She'd seen their faces. Rabid, high on cruelty and chemical stimulation. If they caught her, it would be the end.

She ran, her feet long frozen, her heart long burst, shrieked for help with a voice long gone.

No help came. Or would come. They were herding her, forcing her off the road and into the dark, dead wood.

"You're dead, rich bitch." A pubescent voice shrilled after her, hitting her square between her shoulder blades. Revulsion made her stumble. "You just don't know it yet."

Barely human, hyena-like panting hoots followed, scraping along her nerve endings. Loathing lurched inside her. It wasn't enough to clear the fog of fear. And even the adrenaline was draining out of her. Resignation was already descending on her, would soon paralyze her.

If only she hadn't always avoided ER and emergency surgeries. Perhaps she could have learned to keep part of herself in reserve, cool under fire. This was hopeless, but she didn't have to make it easy for them!

Perhaps if she made it too much trouble to reach her, if she climbed a tree, maybe they'd just go away...?

A lifetime ago she'd been a tree-climber. Another forbidden activity she'd done behind her father's back before every impulse and initiative had been trained out of her. Richardson princesses didn't scrape knees and velvet cheeks. Didn't fall out of trees and sprain precious hands groomed for Prince

5

Charming's five-carat diamond rings and ten-thousand-dollar scalpels.

Richardson princesses also didn't attend the kind of party two of them had gone to tonight. The one she'd just escaped, only to discover she'd run from the fire into an inferno.

One of her stiletto-heeled evening shoes was long lost and her foot was raw. She had to kick off the second to climb.

She didn't even remember how to do it. Her hands and legs trembled so hard she lost her grip and footing. She staggered down the few feet she'd climbed, her backless designer dress catching on the thorny branches, ripping. Her skin was already a red-hot map of lacerations.

Her pursuers were below her now. She hadn't gotten far enough up. Two of them climbed after her, one snatching at her legs, the other at her long dress.

She plummeted to the ground and was only sorry the vicious impact didn't knock her out. She lay at their feet, crumpled, cowering. Then she felt the clawing hands, saw the faces filling her dimming vision. *Let them finish me quickly.*

But instead of falling on her, one of her attackers flew into the air and hit a tree with a sickening crunch. A second assailant turned, only to convulse once and collapse on her in an unmoving heap.

She struggled under his dead weight, her mind frozen with all sorts of impossible fears. What force had come to her rescue? Would it now turn on her?

The body was heaved off her. Suddenly she was free from her burden and saw—him.

Huge, menacing, and emitting power. A man?

"I wouldn't advise you to do that." His voice was like the night, still, deep—heart-stopping.

Not heeding his advice, her regrouping attackers charged him, slashing the air with switchblades. He moved, maneuvered, his arcing legs and arms a dance of precise power. The thugs thudded to the ground one after another.

Then he turned to her. *Dear God.*

"Are you hurt?"

What did that matter as long as he was here?

Her headshake earned her a satisfied nod. Then he took care of business. He called the police and an ambulance for her, and knocked out those thugs who tried to stir, securing them for easy pick-up by the police. Then he stood by her as she gave her statement, supporting her in every way, and tried to get her to have her cuts treated, to call someone.

She just needed to be away from here. With him.

"I have a first-aid kit at home. Will you take me there?"

Everything went still as he stared down at her. If he said no…

He didn't. He held her in the curve of his body all the way to his car, warding off the cold, absorbing the ordeal.

All the way to her apartment she luxuriated in studying him.

She'd never seen anything so beautiful. So perfect.

He carried her to the elevator and into her apartment, stood outside her bathroom as she showered. She'd just slipped into her bathrobe when she saw him there, looming behind her as she stood facing the drug-cabinet mirror, a frown marring his hard, noble features. Her helpless gaze clung to his rich chocolate eyes, his wide, sculpted mouth, saw her feverish awareness reflected there.

Then he pushed her bathrobe down.

Oh, God. Had she just jumped from one inferno into another? If she had, she was fully to blame for this one…

Her fears came to a shamed halt as he reached for the first-aid materials. Then those beautiful hands that had been damaged in her defense were everywhere she hurt, healing, cherishing, until she felt his gentleness sealing her wounds, seeping through to her soul.

How could she have feared him? He had to be an angel. Her own angel.

Now she knew what it meant to want. It was *this*, wanting him.

He draped her again, slipped an analgesic tablet between her lips, held the glass of water to her mouth then stepped away. "Now you need to rest." She closed her eyes and let his magnificent voice permeate her with peace, protection—passion. "Are you sure you won't call someone? A friend? A relative?"

For answer, she just surged into him, burrowed all she could into his chest.

Shock, resistance then control chased through him. His battered hand below her chin raised her eyes to his smile. *Oh, my!* "All right. I'll stay. Let's put you to bed—you need to sleep this off."

"I need to sleep with *you*." There was no question in her mind. None.

He moved away. But not before she felt his powerful, instant response. "*Querida*, you've had the scare of your life. You're shaken, still unable to believe you're safe, that it's over." Those healing hands went to the back of his neck, dug into his silken, raven mane. "You just need a haven, comfort…"

"I need you!"

"No…"

"Yes." Her mind had never been this clear, her focus never this unwavering. She could have died tonight with just stunted, barren relationships to her record, without knowing someone existed who could spread life into her every fiber. But she knew now. This man *would* be her lover. Why wait for later when sooner—now—was here? "You don't need to protect me now. You just need to make love to me."

She dropped her bathrobe to the floor, reached for his proud head, brought it down, pressed her lips to his forehead then pressed his mouth to her breast.

His shaken breath scorched her with a blast of desire, with

his helpless confession of equal craving. "Savannah…" She took her name out of his mouth, tasted his power and his submission, and knew everything she'd done in life had been just another step leading her here.

CHAPTER ONE

"WHAT the *hell* are you doing here?"

Savannah's hand jerked. The Thermos missed her mouth and cold water splashed down her neck, between suddenly prickling breasts.

Not exactly the welcome she'd hoped for.

Not that she'd expected a welcome. Or had even had expectations in the first place. She'd had…projections, possible scenarios. Indifference and maybe some unease played major roles in each. But Javier sounded neither indifferent nor uneasy now. He sounded livid, big time.

A tremulous breath escaped. *You've had three years to prepare for this moment. You should be as ready as can be.*

She should be. But she wasn't.

Turn to him. And stop trembling, for God's sake.

She turned. It was a good thing she had the Jeep to sag back on. Javier was less than a foot away, glowering down at her from his intimidating height, the tropical sun at its zenith throwing stark shadows over his face. Had he always been that hard-hitting?

Yes, he had.

But that…*hard*?

Yeah again, once, that last night together, right before he'd walked out on her.

Oh, she'd missed him!

But that wasn't news. She'd known that, and how much. What she hadn't factored in had been what seeing him again would do to her or how she'd handle it, outwardly at least. A thirty-year-old who hadn't yet mastered basic logic. Result: another miscalculation.

So what was one more in a life made of a string of those? Onwards, then. But since throwing herself into the arms that were pointedly folded across his vast chest was out, she had to try something else. A smile, maybe? Nah. He was liable to answer it with a snarl. And it would just wobble and shatter anyway.

OK, one thing left. *Talk. Something light.* "Nice to see you, too, Javier."

His legs didn't move but his body leaned closer. The balmy Bogotá day suddenly sizzled. "I don't remember saying it was nice to see you, Savannah." His voice lowered, softened, becoming the voice that had rocked her with passion and shattered her with pleasure during long-gone months of abandon. "Since it's definitely not."

She pressed back against the Jeep, itching inside and out with the effort not to press into him, come what may. "Not very polite of you, with me a first-time guest in your country."

"But you're not a guest, Savannah, are you? You're here intruding on my work, on my project, and I want to know why!"

"So I'm not a guest, but more of a pest, huh?"

Was that surprise in those lethal eyes? An unwilling spurt of amusement? She'd once accessed all his senses but never his sense of humor…

His head inclined to one side, his hair following the move, falling over his forehead. "Your words, not mine."

Her hands burned to smooth back the blue-black gloss, expose the expanse of sculpted bronze. Her heart sizzled with regret over the long-lost freedom to reach up and trace his every line with adoring fingers and lips.

A windblast stirred dust off the unpaved road. Her eyes stung.

Oh, no, you don't. It was all over, gone and done with.

Picking up where he'd cut them off wasn't an option on his side. It shouldn't be on hers.

Remember what you're here for. Get this done the right way this time. No doing things out of order.

She straightened away from the Jeep, not adding much to her comparative size but adjusting her swooning stance. "So we're clear on your stand. You'd rather I was in Alaska."

"Not really." *Oh?* "Just back where you belong, and not here, intruding on my territory." *Oh.*

Ridiculous. Wishful. She *knew* he'd rather not have set eyes on her again. How could hope to the contrary even stir—even exist? Was self-delusion immortal? Resurrected over and over, no matter how many times it was laid to rest?

She shrugged. "I see. Oh, well, I didn't expect you'd be exactly happy I'm here. But here I am, and I hope you'll adjust to the new situation—"

The twisting of his mouth interrupted her speech, and her heart. "Take it like a man, get over it, face the facts and all that, huh?"

Teasing? Was he teasing her? The old Javier had never joked with her. He'd never even sensually teased her. After that first time, he'd always met her more than halfway, perpetually eager, devouring, ready—oh, so ready, until she'd grown sure of him, of her power over him, had grown intoxicated with the certainty. Then one horrible night he'd proved how wrong she'd been to feel so secure...

But if he was teasing now, that had to be good, didn't it? Her spirits lifted a bit. "Your words, not mine."

At her mimicry his eyes, which had once been richest chocolate, became opaque rocks of resentment and disgust. So it hadn't been fun after all, but fury, tamed, camouflaged and now bared. "Nice to see you're enjoying yourself. Just like you, to do it at others' expense. But I'll be damned if you do it at my project's. You've made a mistake coming here. Now

save us all a lot of hassle—just head back to Bogotá airport
and take the first flight home.''

She had wished for something other than indifference,
hadn't she? Well, she should have been more specific what
she'd wished for. She wasn't ready for this.

The worst she'd been ready for had been that he'd be uncomfortable, that he'd think that she was still unable to take
no for an answer. *And wouldn't he be right to think so?*

No. Not exactly. And even if he was right, her presence
shouldn't inflame him this way. This went beyond aggravation, the worst the situation arguably deserved. *This* bordered
on hostility.

Why should he be hostile? He might have originally had
cause to be bitter, but as things had progressed, if there had
to be bitterness, it should be on *her* side. He had gotten his
own back, had walked away from her and had turned down
all her pleas for even one last glance.

She squared her shoulders. ''Again, thanks for the lovely
welcome, Javier. It's so good to know how eagerly my par-
ticipation in the mobile surgery unit's mission is anticipated.''

''You could have saved yourself the trip, and the unpleas-
antness, if only you'd checked with me before coming.''

''Oh, sure. You responded promptly to all my past messages, didn't you?''

''If you're trying to say you've contacted me lately, don't!
The last time I received a message from you was exactly two
and a half years ago.''

So—he *had* kept a record of her pathetic attempts. Six
months' worth of them, dozens per day at first, and all met
with scorn and silence. What a time to discover she'd been
hoping her messages had never reached him, that he hadn't
just ignored her.

Had he enjoyed making her grovel?

Maybe. Probably. Fine, that was his prerogative. But she
was done feeling overwhelmed being near him again. And

there'd be no groveling now. She was a legitimate colleague, an equal. He'd better start dishing out the respect she deserved.

"I didn't think I needed to contact you. I wasn't aware I needed your permission."

"You didn't think you owed me the courtesy of asking my opinion about joining *my* project?"

"It's a Global Aid Organization-sponsored project, and they sent you all the details."

The comfortable climate, which still amazed her since they were so near the equator, chilled with the frost in his glance and voice. "I know what GAO sent me. A surprise letter, just yesterday, informing me of the change of plans. "'Dear Dr. Sandoval Noriega…'" His delivery switched to a mock narrator's as he recited from memory. "'This is to *inform* you that Dr. Savannah Richardson is replacing Dr. Rupert Fiennes as your MSU's medical co-administrator for the next two months. She's been selected from a host of *highly qualified* surgeons to represent GAO's interest in your most ambitious project and as an *integral* part of our continued and dedicated sponsorship.'"

The words "highly qualified" and "integral" hit her in the face, his tone an amalgam of insult and wrath. Was that it? Did he think "highly qualified" an exaggeration, even a lie? He thought it beyond her to be "integral" to anything—to anyone—her presence as good as her absence? As she'd been to him…

He was going on. "I know all the details all right. What I'm asking, what you haven't answered, is what *you're* doing here. What happened to Rupert? And just how did you manage to worm your way into this? GAO is supposed to be a humanitarian effort, out of bounds for your profit-based medical empire. How did you pull their strings? Or shouldn't I ask? Hell…" His huff of laughter was all jaded derision. "Between you and your *royal* family, you can pull anything off. So what really remains is why. This isn't your scene, Savannah. Why do this, why come here? Just tell me—why?''

Why?

Javier wanted to roar the word. Rave and rant it.

Why? Why now? When he'd started to forget.

She couldn't be here, doing this, for him. But what other explanation was there? Was that what he was doing? Prodding her into an admission that she was here, pursuing him? Was that what he wanted?

No! He didn't want her anywhere near him. He wanted life to restart before the moment he'd heard her cries, before he'd saved her and doomed himself.

Oh, did he now?

Demonios! Was there no delivery from addiction?

Stupid. Susceptible. *Male.* That was what she'd always made him, boiling him down to his elements, wrenching out and keeping his focus, his lust—his idiocy.

''I…'' Her answer was cut off when her driver came forward, bringing her luggage and papers for her to sign. She brushed against Javier as she advanced towards the man.

He ached—everywhere, every way.

No. He hadn't started to forget. He wouldn't ever, it seemed. But he'd been at a point when he'd ceased to dwell on his cravings and despondency. He'd shoved all that made him male into sealed containment and had gone ahead full force at being a doctor. This had been where he'd been safe from the hunger. No longer, if she was here.

He'd never expected this. This direct invasion of his sanctuary.

How dared she?

His ferocious thoughts roiled with Bogotá's warmer than usual wind, running hot invisible fingers through her hair. It was no longer the waist-length platinum cascade he'd once sheathed himself in, lost his mind in, but just a burnished halo that made her look the angel that she wasn't. Why had she cut it? He'd once begged her never to.

Why should that upset *him*? He'd made his decision and had stuck to it, had walked away. And he'd always known his wishes had never mattered to her. Her being here was more proof of that!

She turned back to him, and the ache became gnawing. But it was only then he noticed. It wasn't only her hair that had changed. Those azure-skies eyes had, too. He couldn't pinpoint how, though. With the rest of her it was easy to pin down the differences. Rich cream had replaced the overall Mediterranean tan. The voluptuous body he'd plundered that first night, and for five delirious months afterwards, possessed a new…resilience? Or was it only because her languorous air was gone? Whatever, she had changed, but not what she still did to him. *Dios!* She *shouldn't* still do this to him.

"He just needed my signature, confirming that I've been delivered into your care. I told him to stick around in case you threw me out on my ear." That was said without that addictive, seductive smile that had always been in her gaze, on her lips. Even during that last confrontation, when it had grated and humiliated, it had still enslaved him. He should be relieved it was gone now, should pray it was gone for ever. He didn't. *El idiota!* "So, you were asking why I'm here. The answer is obvious. To work."

"Excuse me as I stagger under the weight of that revelation. Quit playing games, Savannah. Richardsons don't work in places like this. What happened to your exalted position within the Richardson Health Group? To your crammed social agenda?" *To Mark?* The question boomed in his head but didn't leave his lips. "And just what strings did you pull to get GAO to make you replace Rupert as my second in command?"

"Co-leader, not second in command!"

"Even worse. If you think I'm just going to just say 'Oh, OK', think again!"

Her breathing changed cadence, irresistibly bringing his eyes to her breasts. Those breasts—the first part of her he'd kissed, when she'd dragged him into an unknown dimension of carnal excess and sensual overload. Even under her utilitarian beige outfit he could detail them. Or was he seeing them through the X-ray of memory?

His body lurched against the shackles of clothes, common sense and control. It had never had doubts. It had always wanted hers, had been punishing him for three years for denying it.

Her hands wiped down her hips then went up to smooth white-gold strands from her eyes. "I don't need to think again, Javier. I *know* firsthand how immovable you are once you've made up your mind. But this time, it's not up to you. You need a co-coordinator, someone with a surgical repertoire to complement yours. Rupert has become unavailable due to a family emergency, and GAO thinks I'm the best replacement and the one qualified to jointly lead this mission with you. They sent me here, they want me here, and here is where I'm staying!"

Shrill honks, laboring motors and clamoring humanity filled the air, the usually ignored soundtrack of the seedier part of Bogotá around the public hospital where he'd been working for the last year. Now it pounded inside his skull, along with the resounding echo of her challenge.

She was staying. She *couldn't* stay.

She had to leave him alone, leave him his work, leave him something unspoiled by her shadow. This was what he'd worked for since Bibiana, every day of the last six years. Then every day and night for the three years since he'd left *her*. She couldn't come now and be part of it. She couldn't *want* to be part of it…

Suddenly it made sense. Yes. That had to be it. "Your

corporation has been behind—how much of the MSU's funding? Since GAO has suddenly been able to answer all my financial requests, I'd say a lot. And you're here to safeguard your corporation's investment, aren't you? You've been sent to road-test the MSU, the prototype, no doubt to give the go-ahead for a future commercial fleet, haven't you?''

Her eyes widened, then narrowed and lowered. What was it that had marred that amazing crystalline blue before they'd dropped? Indignation? Hurt?

No way was it hurt. She had to care to be hurt. And she didn't care. She never had. Not about him, not about anything.

But why should there be indignation either, if it was the truth? So maybe it wasn't…

No! It had to be the truth.

Savannah kept her eyes averted, bracing herself against the slap of Javier's disparagement. *Ha, what a fool!*

She'd been fishing all along, looking for signs of personal involvement in his antagonism. Well, he'd sure put her straight.

His resentment had nothing personal about it. He just had a low opinion of her, as low as his expectations for his life's work were high. He hated the idea of combining the two. Had he always felt like that? Had he always seen all her shortcomings when she'd thought she'd blinded him to them? But in accusing her of coming to commercialize his noble plans, soiling his pure purpose, he'd invented a fault she'd never had.

Of all the holier-than-thou nerve!

''Listen, Javier, I'm sure you and your prejudices and self-satisfaction are very happy together, but I'll just have to disappoint you. I'm here in the same capacity as you are. The success of the MSU's mission is my only objective, and not as a part of a marketing plan. You can believe what you like and keep your precious Latin chauvinism intact, or you can check my credentials with GAO—''

"Are you saying you're *with* GAO? Not a representative of your corporation and holding GAO by the purse strings?"

"And I always thought you had an impressive IQ. Guess I was wrong!"

"If *I'm* wrong, can you tell me what you think you're doing here, joining a mission that will take us on the road in some of the most conflict-ridden regions in the country, a country that's an open stage for guerrilla wars, escalating urban violence, and widespread poverty? Into danger and filth and desperation, with the bare necessities alone, for two months? You wouldn't last two days!"

He was probably right.

No. She wasn't starting out by doubting herself, undermining her resolve. If he could do it, so could she.

Really?

Oh, she didn't know. But that was why she was here. To find out. Find everything out. Once and for all.

She looked up into eyes made alien by harsh mockery and repressed anger, wondered again how much she deserved all the harsh, disparaging thoughts flitting through them. Then she raised one eyebrow and issued a challenge that was all bravado. "We'll see, won't we?"

"No, we won't, Savannah." Suddenly he wasn't hostile or angry any more, just grim with conviction. "This isn't some reality TV show where help is always within reach and danger is manufactured, and you can pull out of the game when you've had enough. The stakes are real here, and once we're on the road we'll be on our own and we'll have to keep going until it's over. You'll just be a burden and a liability. Look at you." His gesture and grimace demonstrated his brutal, irrevocable judgment far more clearly than words. "Whatever your reasons for being here, they're invalid and all your expectations are ridiculous. For everyone's and everything's sake, *go home*."

Savannah felt her heart dry and her lungs empty.

Everyone believed she'd wither like some delicate plant if removed from her pot of affluence and privilege. She had strong doubts herself, yet that had only spurred her, motivated her.

But Javier dismissing her as deadweight to be abandoned for everyone's welfare, a black hole to be escaped at all costs—was that what she truly was? Was that what she'd been to him? That didn't spur her on, didn't motivate her. That just hurt. Crippled.

Oh, God, don't let him see how much.

God heard her. The tropical sky, clear just minutes ago, darkened then wept, obscuring her tears.

Two hours later, Savannah was lying flat on her back, staring through throbbing eyes around the clean, spartan room Javier had given her. Just to shower and change out of her drenched clothes, he'd stressed. Then she was going.

His room. His bed. His presence permeated everything there, clung—clawed.

So the hold he'd had on her senses hadn't lessened. It had all been real, none of it exaggerated through time and absence. The breath in her lungs was laden with his scent. She forced it out on a moan of arousal and crushing shame.

What was she doing here? Had she really come here of her own choice? Worked for this, fought for this? Had she finally lost it?

It was a good thing Javier was being sane enough for both of them. He was shipping her home, and she was grateful.

A familiar melody filtered to her ears. It had been droning on and off in the background, calling, insistent… Oh, damn, her cell phone!

She didn't want to answer it. It would be her father. Or Mark. Or Lucas. Her watchdogs. She had nothing to say to any of them.

After the ninth interminable ring, she succumbed. Maybe they were worried…

No, they weren't. They would have minute-by-minute updates of her movements on each of their desks by now. They were just being their usual looking-over-her-shoulder nuisance selves.

She answered. It was her father. That figured. The man believed at an unreasoning level that she was thirteen and not thirty. There was no point contesting a lost cause, though. Not when she'd already supplied him with a dozen proofs for his case against her.

She told him everything. He'd find out on his own sooner rather than later anyway. Jacob Richardson had mystical ways of being in the know. She didn't even attempt to hide her distress. She was sick of pretending to be her old blasé self, tired of keeping up the invulnerable façade she'd been sporting since Javier had left her. She wasn't OK and she no longer cared if it distressed her father to know it. He couldn't think any less of her anyway.

"I *haven't* changed my mind!" She was damned if she'd admit to him, of all people, that she was sort of relieved Javier had beaten her back, relieved at being forced to relinquish a coveted but much-feared ambition—the relief of closure. "But Javier flat out refuses to work with me." Sad sarcasm twisted her lips at her father's answering indignation. Even when Javier was fulfilling her father's desires by aborting her mission, the older man begrudged it that he was the one to achieve it. Javier had always pushed his buttons—and those of every other man she knew, for that matter. "Javier Sandoval thinks himself exactly what he is: the project's director, and I— Aah!"

Her alarmed cry at Javier bursting into the room was followed by her father's frantic shouts. *For heaven's sake—end this.* "No, Daddy, nothing's wrong. Someone just rushed in and startled me." A moment while her father probed and prodded again. "No, I don't *want* to go, Daddy. *Daddy.* I'll call later. Bye."

She cut the connection, let the cell phone fall from her nerveless fingers as her eyes clashed with Javier's across the small space.

He'd see it all. Her defeat, the fresh anguish her father's scolding had managed to squeeze out of her, the way she was curled around his pillow, as she'd once curled around him...

So what? Let him see. Let him have his victory.

He came closer. Was that how he looked when he was triumphant? As he looked down at the huddled, spent body of his adversary, his conquest? Fierce, beautiful—unreadable.

She'd never really understood him. Or known him. Their five incendiary months together had been consumed in an insatiable conflagration. Had it been any wonder only ashes had remained? That he'd left her as easily as a stranger?

A shake of his head dismissed her yet again, snapped the moment. He moved rapidly to the other side of the room, opened a locked closet and produced a box. Surgical instruments! Was there need for them? An emergency?

The possibility of someone in need, of being of use, dispersed all her self-pity and lethargy. "What is it?"

Her question earned her a quick glance and nothing else. She could see the box. A stent graft kit. In seconds she was running beside him down the corridor. "A ruptured abdominal aortic aneurysm?"

His surprised glance raised her temperature. If he dared ask how she knew...!

"The stent graft kit." He named her clue, answering his own unvoiced astonishment. "Yes. It's Garcia, one of our janitors."

"Have you done CT, MRIs?"

"No time. He's collapsed already."

"Did he have aneurysm history, or is this *de novo*?"

"If you're asking indirectly how I know what I'm talking

about, it's because Garcia was kind enough to have the classical clinical triad of ruptured AAA—hypotension, pulsatile abdominal mass and back pain. He even vomited and fainted just to underline the diagnosis. He's also seventy years old and an ex-heavy smoker. So it all adds up. Anyway, all investigative methods aren't reliable in detecting a ruptured AAA."

She knew that. And if the clinical picture was that solid, it would be criminal to delay intervention to obtain time-consuming diagnostic proof. "Is OR ready?"

"As we speak. And why do you ask?"

"I want to assist!"

"I have my surgical nurse already in OR, scrubbed and ready."

"I don't believe this. I don't believe *you*! You have your choice of a surgeon and a surgical nurse for your first assistant, and you choose the nurse?"

"She's highly trained—"

"As opposed to me, of course!"

He gave an impatient grunt. "She knows my protocols, my methods, anticipates my moves…"

"Great. An experienced instrument and circulating nurse is absolutely necessary for the efficiency of the operation."

"*And* as effective as an MD in an aneurysm surgery. A second surgeon is *not* required for the first assistant position here—"

"So get it through your thick head," she completed for him. "You're neither needed nor wanted, so just go away." Her feet stumbled, changed direction and started running back. *Just get me out of here.*

Heavy footsteps immediately thundered after her, caught up with her at the door to his room. He yanked her around, almost shook her once, a gesture eloquent with exasperation. Then he dragged her back, had her running and stumbling after him all the way to the scrubbing and gowning area. He released her there, his eyes averted, his agitation resonating with hers as they got ready. They strode into OR, Javier holding the swing door open for her with his back to it. As she passed him, he extended his elbow in her path, stopping her.

His noble, tough face was tense. So was his voice. "We never worked together."

No. Neither had they eaten together, or shopped or laughed or chatted or quarreled, or even *slept* together. They'd just made love. Then they'd just parted. He'd just gone.

"I know. It'll be all right."

Javier found himself nodding and following her inside, making lightning introductions, assigning chores to his OR staff, maneuvering her to his first assistant's position.

What had gotten into him? This was an emergency. Every second counted. So what was he doing, substituting versatile, ultra-efficient Anita for Savannah, an unknown quantity at best? The title of surgeon didn't automatically endow her with the full range of abilities expected of a competent one. Not when she'd come by it with her medical mogul father's help.

It was too late now. It had been too late since he'd heard her voice break back in that corridor. Before that even, when he'd found her huddled and tear-stained in his bed. Or when not even the tropical shower had hidden her unprecedented tears. Adding vulnerability to her arsenal of feminine weapons had accessed every soft, gullible, terminally male weakness he had—and he couldn't afford to give in to them.

No matter now. If anything went wrong, he'd just have to handle it as the primary surgeon, reshuffle positions as the situation warranted.

"Pressure 80 over 60." Savannah said, addressing Anita. "He needs more fluid resuscitation. Continue saline delivery until systolic BP is a hundred."

Anita's black eyes narrowed on her, then turned to Javier. He was aware of Savannah's eyes following the communication. She inclined her head whimsically. "It's called 'hypotensive hemostasis'. We give the patient enough fluids to correct his circulatory collapse, while not raising his pressure enough to cause an increase in bleeding from the rupture, or to dilute his blood and clotting factors.''

That was the perfect rationale and the clearest explanation! A point for her theoretical knowledge. He nodded his agreement to Anita who implemented Savannah's directions at once.

But he wasn't surprised to find that part of her knowledge solid. During their time in the same teaching hospital, he'd learned she had an aptitude for information-gathering and processing, the talent that had got her straight As all through her education. But she also combined that skill with no desire whatsoever to apply her knowledge. In his opinion, that made her worse than a knowledge-deficient yet committed doctor. Ready and assured surgical prowess wasn't as easy to achieve as memorizing textbooks. It took relentless application, nerve, and a lot of caring for one's patients. All of which she'd lacked.

Savannah pressed closer as he started the procedure. ''Since Garcia is just sedated, and since you've run for stent grafts, I assume you're attempting an endovascular repair first?''

He injected the local anesthetic block of the femoral nerve. ''Yes. I won't risk the high morbidity and mortality associated with open surgical repair as long as Garcia hasn't entered frank circulatory collapse yet. I have to try minimally invasive routes first.''

''Ah, what you're famous for.'' She remembered that? Strange. He'd believed she'd never really registered anything about him.

Savannah took the empty anesthetic syringe from him, handed him the scalpel. ''In Richardson Memorial, endovascular grafts, combined with hypotensive hemostasis and other endovascular techniques, including proximal balloon control, have become the norm in treating ruptured AAAs.''

Had they now? And she kept abreast with the latest developments and trends? "Have you participated in any yourself?"

"I did a few during my stint in vascular surgery, early fifth residency year. Six, to be exact."

Oh. "Elective aneurysm repair?"

"Ruptured ones. From leaking to catastrophic. Four are still alive two years later."

Could she be exaggerating? That was an impressive result by any standards, since more than fifty per cent of treated ruptured AAAs died of complications within thirty days of surgery. Not to mention those who died intra-operatively, or even before that.

He opened his mouth to ask for the guide-wire, but Savannah was already handing it to him. He stared at her, at a loss for a second. Shaking himself, he turned to Anita. "Prepare for arteriography."

Anita handed him the contrast material injection, the radio-opaque solution that would make the artery visible in X-ray imaging, showing the exact position where the aorta was abnormally dilated into an aneurysm, and the point where it had ruptured. The OR technician maneuvered the arteriographic X-ray machine overhead.

Javier made the incision into the skin and subcutaneous fat of the groin. Savannah anticipated his request for tissue retraction and helped him gain exposure of the femoral artery. He introduced the guide-wire into the artery and advanced it until he entered the supracoeliac aorta under X-ray guidance, watching his progress on the monitor.

"What if the aorto-iliac anatomy isn't suitable for stent grafting?"

Her question brought his eyes back to her. It was an advanced bit of vascular surgery knowledge to understand that if the artery was kinked or narrowed before the dilation of the aneurysm, it was out of the question to repair the rupture by grafting the intra-arterial prosthesis inside the aorta, holding it in place by metal braces or stents. Maybe she hadn't been exaggerating her experience after all.

"Let's hope Garcia continues to be a textbook case, Savannah."

And he was. He had perfect aortic anatomy—except for the ruptured aneurysm. After Javier introduced the balloon catheter into the artery he found himself saying, "Would you like to do it?"

Savannah jerked up in surprise, her stunning eyes, all he could see of her now, settling on him for an eloquent second. *Dios!* He couldn't believe his hardening body, here, now!

"Sure." Savannah's hand took over his grip on the catheter, then with steady, practiced movements, she expanded the metal stent to fit against the inside of the aorta, reinforcing its wall and holding the synthetic sleeve in place, bridging and sealing the rupture. No doubt now. She'd done this many times before, and had done it well.

After checking the stability of their graft, they worked together as if they'd been doing so all their lives, closing up, placing drains in Garcia's abdomen to siphon off the blood that had collected there and auto-infusing it back into him after washing and filtering it through a cell-saver device. Afterwards they re-checked his vitals, topped off his sedation and analgesia, then accompanied him to Intensive Care.

Javier walked out of IC behind Savannah, the elation of a surgery well performed and a coworker saved fading, confusion and agitation replacing it, warring for dominance in his chest.

Sending Savannah away had been a simple matter of pragmatism before. Or that would have been his argument. She was unqualified, on all counts, period.

He'd been wrong on one count, the one that mattered most. She was surgically competent. So what excuse could he give GAO—worse, give *her*—as he looked her in the eye and told her to leave? His belief that she would melt in the heat of toil and discomfort was only his opinion. No one, starting with her, was bound to take it.

So what could he say? That he couldn't function with her around? That his mind had emptied of everything but the need to drag her back to his room, rip her out of her clothes and bury himself in her, take her, then take her again until he'd made up for just the first few days of the three years without her?

They reentered his room and he leaned on the door, his hormones roaring with every move she made. Then she turned to him and had him ready to relinquish all sanity, just standing there. It had to be witchcraft. Mind-bending and ruinous…

"Do you still want me to leave, Javier?"

No! Don't leave. You're all wrong and damaging and out of my league. But stay. Stay until you've finished me.

His pager went off. *Gracias Dios!*

He walked out without a word.

Savannah fell to the bed, her eyes feeling like hot gravel, her chest a smoldering coal. What a mistake it had been, coming here. It had to be her last with him. Any more would finish her.

"'Do you still want me to leave, Javier?'"

Her heart lurched in her throat at hearing her own words, mockingly repeated like a slowed-down tape. She jerked up.

Javier. It was only Javier.

But in the next split second, her relief froze into dread at witnessing what filled his eyes. Hatred.

"'I don't *want* to go, Daddy.'" He mimicked her again, the loathing deepening. "And *Daddy* made sure you wouldn't, didn't he?"

"Wh-what are you talking about?"

He held up a paper in front of her eyes, let it go. It tumbled into her lap, as he snarled at her. "I'm talking about *this*!"

CHAPTER TWO

"THIS is a delightful piece of coercion, isn't it?"

Savannah's eyes avoided the venom in Javier's, ran over the fax.

He went on. "Did you dictate it over the phone? Or did you leave it up to 'Daddy' and his legal bloodhounds?"

She struggled to make sense of the convoluted legal language and missed half of it. But one thing shrieked at her, without the least pretense of finesse or the usual legal euphemisms, overbearing, openly threatening.

If she went, so did GAO's backing of the MSU and its missions.

Oh, damn! Who was responsible for this?

What kind of a fool question was that? Her father, of course. He'd probably got Mark to take care of the arm-twisting, and Lucas of the paper- and legwork.

But *why*?

Even though she'd told her father that going back wouldn't mean going back to *him*, it had to be a step in the right direction in his opinion. He'd have her where he could continue to work on her until she gave in, rejoined the ranks and became once more part of the sparkling display he'd been pushing her to be since the day she'd been born.

So why make it possible for her to stay away? And here, of all places?

Only one thing could have made him do this. His abhorrence of Javier! And it seemed that telling him about Javier's refusal to work with her had suggested the perfect way to get back at the man he'd hated to see on her mind and in her bed.

No matter what, Javier Sandoval didn't boss Jacob Richardson's daughter around.

But there was more. It was all congealing into one ugly piece of insight.

Following the workings of her father's elitist mind and looking through his manipulative eyes, this had to be an all-objectives-achieved coup. He'd drive Javier to the ground, tower over him and show him who was boss, and *then* his fragile daughter would get all uncomfortable and miss her Jacuzzi and pedicurist's services and run home on her own.

This last bit of rationalization had to be why he'd stopped fighting her over coming to Colombia in the first place. *Oh, let the headstrong girl have her way. Resist her and she'll play the martyr. Let her go and she'll be back with her tail between her legs in no time.*

All in all, a perfect set-up.

No wonder Javier was boiling. If not as much as she was.

Daddy dearest had a call coming all right. A wake-up call. It was finally time to give him a crash course on the lines she wouldn't let him cross. Maybe she was as fragile as they both thought she was, and she *had* let him push her around all her life, but she was damned if she'd let him push Javier around, too!

"I believe this belongs to me." Javier's bronzed fingers eased the fax out of hers with great restraint. "I'm sure you'll get, or you already have, your own copy."

She clung to his hand, stopped him as he stepped away. "I won't—I don't. Javier, this isn't my doing!"

Insistent, controlled strength took him out of her reach, his considering glance moving like a sweep of acid across her skin. She would rather he'd slapped her. "It never is, is it?"

"What do you mean?"

"I mean with you it's always someone else's doing, some-one else's fault. Your mother made you get engaged to Jordan, your friends convinced you Andrew was the man for you, then your father decreed you were made for Mark, his protégé and heir apparent. Belinda *made* you go to the party from hell, then someone there *made* you escape it, then—''

''Then I *made* you come to my rescue, then *made* you sleep with me. It seems some things are my doing after all.''

''None of that was 'doing', just reacting.''

''And what was your excuse?''

''None. I was reacting, too. But I stopped.''

Yeah, he had, hadn't he? Just like that. He'd decided there and then that it had been time to stop ''reacting'', to start acting. He'd stepped out of her bed, had left her there still quivering with his last explosive pleasuring, and had never looked back. And he was now rubbing it in that *she'd* never stopped to think of the consequences of her ''reactions''. And she hadn't, certainly not with him. Not then, not now.

He was also telling her what she'd been to him. A knee-jerk reaction, an impulse it had taken a moment's clarity to grow sick of, to walk away from.

Did he know he'd found the best method of hurting her?

If he was out to do that, she couldn't blame him. He must think she was doing the same, messing up his life's ambition, what he'd invested all his fortune and time and aspiration in. But it was so ambitious that he'd needed help, and had spent six years slaving for the kind of unconditional support that would leave him in charge and wouldn't exploit his success or corrupt his purpose.

Now he'd been made aware that all his work had been in vain, that he wasn't really in charge and would never be, that conditions could be made at random and new terms invented, that someone could yank his strings and his project's as and when their whims dictated.

Impotence and wrath and humiliation must have eaten him through to the bone by now.

The only way to absorb his fury was to tell him that he

could shred that fax, kick her out and nothing would happen, that it was an empty threat, that she'd make sure it was.

But would that be enough? Would he forget the slap? Could he go on from here pretending not to see the leash now he knew it existed?

She had to try. "Javier, let's not make this personal—"

"I beg to differ. Let's. It's very personal to me after all—though I'm sure you can't possibly know what *that* feels like."

She took a moment to wait out the sting. "Maybe—but I do know how *you* feel, how personal this is to you. It was the only thing you ever talked to me about, so I know. But this ultimatum—it isn't going to happen. Whatever legal mumbo jumbo this says, it won't come to pass. If I leave, GAO's backing won't be following me."

"How kind of you to *grant* me this."

"I'm not granting you anything. My father has interfered again, unasked and unfairly—"

"*Unfairly?* Unfair is when he gave you a two-mile private beach on the Caribbean and gave his new wife a ten-mile one. This I call coercive, fraudulent, unethical—even criminal."

"I won't make excuses for him. There are none."

"Very gracious of you."

"Oh, please! Listen, Javier, you have every right to be angry, every right to feel insulted, oppressed and threatened. But I will reverse this."

He recoiled from the hand that touched his muscled arm, moved to the door. Oh, no. He wasn't walking away before she'd had her say this time.

She ran round him, spread her arms across the door. He'd have to go through her if he wanted to get out.

His arms spread out, too, echoing his frustrated expression. "Haven't I already expressed my gratitude that you will call your dogs off? Now I have work to do. The MSU won't be deployed on its own, you know."

"They're not my dogs! But I'll make sure nothing like this ever happens again, not from anyone I know. I understand it won't be much of a consolation, even if they swear in binding documents that they'll never spring ultimatums on you again. The memory that they've dictated to you and could have gotten away with it won't go away soon. I *am* truly sorry that I can't erase that. But maybe through my own efforts, I can atone for it."

Oh, God, why was he looking at her that way? As if she'd grown a new pair of eyes?

Just say this, put your cards on the table.

She had to breathe first, before she blacked out. "I came here to work, Javier…" She paused for another breath. "And for many other reasons, too. I joined GAO a year ago, trained hard and worked locally with them. But I did have my eye on this project of yours. How could I not when I'd heard so much about it from you? I didn't think they'd give me such an important mission on my first time out, but they think I'm qualified for this, and I want to see if they're right, to see this through. I want to be of use and of service, and maybe make that little bit of a difference, too. But I don't want to be here against your wishes. I won't be. It *is* up to you whether I stay or go. If you really think the MSU's mission would be better off without me, if you have someone else in mind who's better qualified and who's more motivated, say so now and I will go. Just promise you won't let anger answer for you."

Savannah's words washed over Javier, drowned his fury, flooded his thoughts.

Who was this woman?

Was this the same woman he'd known in total intimacy? She had the same voice, the same body, the same brutal attraction. But was that the same character? The same mind?

The mind he remembered had been focused on fashion and entertainment trivia, on hedonistic pleasures. By necessity it had also contained the medical information that had seen her through medical school and the first three years of residency, but that, along with every relevant thing, had been undetectable. Or had that been his clouded perception? Had this mind always inhabited the body he'd worshipped, and it had been him who'd been too inflamed to see beyond the sexual promise?

Maldita sea—he'd never even heard her talk so much, and certainly not in such an ordered or impassioned way. She'd always said little, communicated less, and had then just conveyed how alien they'd been to one another. The rest had been lost in frenzied passion. Or had it been him who'd never given her the chance to say much, with his hands and lips and body all over her, bent on making her as breathless for him as he'd been for her?

No, he didn't think so. So had she changed? Grown up? But could anyone simply develop the kind of insight that had analyzed his feeling of oppression, and the logic and delicacy that had defused it?

This was looking worse by the second. For if the frivolous girl she'd been had twisted him around her finger, what would a more complex woman do to him?

Ah, Dios, why had she come?

She wanted to stay, to work, she'd said. And for many other reasons, too. What reasons? Was he among them? And if he was, then as what? There'd only ever been one thing between them. Sex. Was it what she still wanted from him? Did he want her to want it from him?

Who was he kidding? Wanting her, wanting her to want him was the only thing he was sure of, no matter how wrong, how pointless and destructive it was, or how hard he fought against it.

"So what do you say, Javier? Just put me out of my misery, OK?"

His eyes swung back to her, found her sitting on the bed

flushed and expectant and ripe. Waiting for his verdict. *Put her out of her misery. And yourself.*

He pushed her flat on her back in his mind, and she writhed to the floor. He followed, his body and his tongue thrusting at her heat, in her mouth, his hands finding her, driving her to her first climax. Then she begged him, for him, and he gave her, almost clothed, almost violent, as she loved him to be that first time, just pushing inside her, pounding her to completion. Then he turned her…

He turned away, his fists pressing his head, pushing back the crushing pressure of lust as he half fell down in the only chair in his tiny room.

He'd almost climaxed just looking and craving. He shouldn't have left himself to starve till now, he should have taken sustenance where it had been offered, where it was still offered.

But nothing would have been sustenance, not after Savannah. Savannah who was here again, the never-ending feast he'd deprived himself of. And he still would. Nothing had changed or, if it had, had only changed for the worse.

Just tell her she can stay. She'll leave soon enough on her own.

He rubbed his face, pressed eyes that felt swollen, inflamed, like the rest of him. Then he rose to stand over her as she leaned back on the bed. She looked as if he'd ravaged her for real, ready for more, for anything…

Dios. This was going to be impossible.

Get it over with, then get out.

"Welcome to Colombia and the MSU mission, Savannah." He swallowed the rasp blocking his breathing. "I hope you've made the right decision coming here. MSU reconnaissance tomorrow at ten a.m. sharp. You can stay here till then."

Savannah watched him turn away, her eyes clinging to his every move as he left the room. The door clicked behind him and the smooth sound ricocheted along her nerves with the force of a close-range bullet. She jerked, sagged back, hurting, her thighs pressing together, desperate to silence the cries and stop the melting.

She'd sat there talking to him, feeling her mind splitting in two. One mind that had her saying all the sane, right things while the other had urged her to writhe against him until she'd made him drag her to the floor, mount her, feed her hunger, release all of his inside her…

She'd been deluding herself, thinking she could be near him and not lose her mind again.

So much for keeping on the right track!

"This is all out of order!"

"It's GAO's schematics that are out of order." Javier's answer came from a foot above and behind her, lazy, deep, maddening—in every way. "This is the new and best functional layout for the MSU."

Savannah looked around once more. *Nothing* was where it belonged. Nothing looked as it should. All those days spent poring over obsolete schematics! All that detailed knowledge she couldn't impress him with! He'd changed the whole place out of recognition.

Frustration burst out of her. "Just when did you do that? When did you have all the changes manufactured and installed? And why didn't you update GAO's database on the specifications of the MSU, or at least notify them of what you were doing? Do you know how much time I spent learning every in and out of the place? A place that no longer—that *never* existed?"

He unfolded one of the stations and sat down, his eyebrows rising at each notch up in her tone, at each sentence that merged into the last, until they disappeared into the lush hair that gleamed navy blue under the MSU's overhead fluorescent lights.

Incredulous, was he? And was that amusement, too? Was it? Ooh…

Four storming footsteps took her to him, a bend at the waist pushed her face into his. Her fists balled on her hips, daring him to twitch those lips once. "Are you enjoying this? Are you? Is that a smile? Huh, is it?"

Her intimidation worked like a charm all right. He burst out laughing.

She'd never seen him laugh. Not once. She'd seen him smile, smolder, frown. She'd heard him drawl, whisper, roar in ecstasy, but never, ever laugh.

Could there be anything more beautiful? Could she last much longer before she just grabbed and devoured him?

She threw her hands in the air. "Yeah, laugh, why don't you? You're not the one who's expected to co-direct this mission while asking everyone you're supposed to direct what and where everything is! You're not the director who needs directions!"

Another boom of laughter greeted her laments, had her sagging against the stainless-steel lining of the MSU's interior. Inciting his laughter was powerful. It could be addictive. She wanted more of it.

She went after more. "And what are all those unlabeled cabinets and multitude of identical panels? What does *your* MSU really stand for? Maze of Similar Unknowns? Mislaid, Slapdash and Unorganized?" She paused for inspiration and a critical, teasing look up and down his awesome, shaking body. "Male: Species Uncertain?"

That brought on a fit of spluttering and choking.

She stood watching him wiping tears and coughing at the mock-severe face she pulled. Oh, what was the use? She'd do it sooner or later anyway. And sooner looked good.

"Right, well, there's one way to shut you up, or save you from laughing yourself to death. Come here."

Her hands bunched on his shoulders, tugged slowly at his

shirt collar. She felt his surprise. Satisfaction leapt through her as she savored every expression that fast-forwarded across his face. Then she sealed his half-open lips, taking her gasped name and his scalding breath into her.

Javier. From the first moment. Everything about him, everything with him had been beyond reason, way out of bounds of right and wrong. He'd warranted one-off rules. Still did. And it had been so long without this, without *him*. No reason was good enough for that kind of deprivation. Had he suffered, too?

Tell me…

Her tongue glided along his lower lip, her teeth and lips following, biting, suckling, anxious for his taste and heat, for his surrender, his dominance.

Tell me!

His body told her first, with a relentless thrust against the thigh that pressed between his. His hand spoke in spasms of passion in her hair, dragging her down, closer. His legs continued the confession, rough, urgent, spreading hers, his other hand beneath her buttocks bringing her where contact was a necessity. Then his lips started telling her the rest…

"Ahem!"

The mockery hit Javier first. Then the realization. Of what he was doing, what he'd let himself in for.

Savannah hadn't heard, it seemed, was still offering her mouth and her body to him, ready for anything he had in mind. He still had his mouth open on hers, his body still surging, unmindful of the intruders. *Push her away.*

He did, watched shock and disappointment clouding her stormy-skies eyes and almost pulled her back. The others would leave, eventually.

He'd gone mad. Again.

He swept them both up to their feet, kept his body in front of hers, blocking the avid glances of his colleagues and giving her time to come down and pull herself together.

"You're late!"

His bark sent his crew members' eyebrows shooting up. What were they so surprised about? It was almost eleven a.m. They *were* late, and it was because they were that this had happened. If they'd been on time, he wouldn't have been alone with Savannah, wouldn't have ended up almost taking her in the first five minutes of this damned mission.

At least they'd made it here when they had. Ten more minutes and they would have walked in on a far more X-rated scene.

Would he have gone all the way? Here? Would he really have been unable to stop? *Yes, you would have. Yes, really,* his body moaned.

"Cool it, Jav!" That was Alonso Carreira, his mission anesthetist, and regrettably his best friend, the one who'd announced their presence. The *double entendre* only spiked Javier's heat even more. "No need to knock us out. One almost out-of-it crew member is enough for one day. That's why we were late."

"It's my fault really." Caridad Dominguez, one of his two surgical nurses, spoke up, her tranquil voice more subdued than normal, her brown eyes lifeless. "I felt a bit faint and everyone insisted I rest before I got on my feet again."

"Gave us quite a scare until she was, too." Alonso winked at him. "Who would have handled sandwiches if we had to go without Cari?"

Caridad's pensive eyes fixed on Alonso for a few seconds. It almost had Javier smacking the smaller man's thick head. The woman loved him! It was a mystery why, when the insensitive wretch kept teasing and tormenting her, oblivious to what he was doing to her.

"Let's take a look at you, Caridad." Javier opened one of the unlabeled cabinets that had confounded Savannah, brushing against her as she headed towards Caridad. His still throbbing body jerked. *Down, amigo.*

Caridad shook her head, looking even worse. "I'm fine, Dr. Sandoval, really."

Savannah shook her head. "Not with that gray tinge to your complexion, you're not!" She steered her to the emergency stretcher, the one thing that wasn't folded inside the unit at the moment. "C'mon, hop up."

"You're the American doctor Javier told us about, Dr.— Dr...."

Miguel de Oliveira, their trauma surgeon, groped for Savannah's name until Elvira, their obstetric surgeon and his wife, came to his rescue. "Dr. Savannah Richardson! It's great to have another woman surgeon along. Another woman, period. We're grossly outnumbered on this mission!"

"How can fourteen men outnumber three women?" Luis Marques, their pediatric surgeon, looked at Javier, inviting his corroboration of his question.

Javier gave it to him. "They can't."

"The boss has spoken." That was their oldest crew member, their driver, guide and security chief, the intimidating Esteban.

Alonso grinned at Elvira. "And now you've become four, you've outnumbered *us*. So, Javier, you were welcoming Dr. Richardson, showing her some homegrown Colombian hospitality, huh?"

Javier glared at Alonso and considered wiping the mischief off his narrow, tanned face.

It was Savannah who answered. "Uh, we were more like catching up. We go way back—sort of."

Sort of, indeed! How cool and practiced. But why should that burn him? He'd known that already.

She turned to him, avoiding his eyes, taking the sphygmomanometer and thermometer from him. Then she returned to Caridad. "Cari—can I call you Cari? Though Caridad is a beautiful name. What does it mean? I get the impression all Spanish names have a meaning."

Caridad blinked at Savannah's rapid words. "Charity."

"Lovely! Just like you."

A tremulous smile broke over Caridad's face, answering Savannah's enthusiasm. "*Gracias!* And your name?"

Savannah finished recording Caridad's BP, and put the thermometer in her mouth as she took her pulse. "Some kind of tropical grassland. I'll never understand what my parents were thinking when they called me that. With my complexion and coloring, I'm more of a tundra!"

It was a testament to everyone's good English that they all understood the joke and laughed in appreciation, each joining in with a comment or an anecdote. Then introductions went round and the scene that had greeted the crew's entrance was dismissed.

Javier watched Savannah chatting, fitting in. Sparkling. *Over*-sparkling. Shaken. So—she wasn't cool at all.

That's better. Something loosened inside him.

In minutes he'd sent everyone off with final directions before departure, and was turning to join Savannah and Elvira who'd been continuing Caridad's check-up. Everything tensed inside him again when Savannah met him halfway, then twisted when she put her hand on his arm.

"I don't get it. She has all the signs of heat exhaustion, bordering on heatstroke." Her open face was serious, engrossed, her whisper audible to him alone. "But Bogotá's climate is so mild, it can't be more than 75 out there."

"Maybe it's just fever."

She shook her head. "I really don't think so. The others said she vomited and collapsed then looked confused and disoriented. She still is, I think. Her blood pressure is low, her temperature is 106 and her mouth is bone dry. I've put her on hyperthermia and rehydration treatment—cooling packs, saline fluid replacement. And Elvira has undressed her and turned up the MSU's air-conditioning." She gave a shudder. "As you must have noticed."

Javier looked back to the prostrate Caridad, realization dawning on him. *"Maldita sea!* Caridad's father had a stroke recently. He works in a glass factory. I remember her saying she and her older brothers would take turns filling in for him so he doesn't lose his job. She must have finished her shift at the furnace then, no doubt, took her siblings to school, carrying the two youngest and towing the rest."

Savannah's eyes became aquamarine with sympathy as they swung back towards Caridad. "Big family?"

"Even bigger than mine."

"She has more than *seven* brothers and sisters?"

That still overwhelmed her, didn't it? And how could it ever cease to? It must be outrageous, even criminal in Savannah's eyes that people should have so many kids, especially under the conditions in this country. Even without those, the idea of so many siblings must be weird, even repulsive to an only child like her.

Just another thing stressing how alien to him she was and would always be.

He nodded. "Eleven. And about a dozen nephews and nieces."

"All in the same house?"

"Around and about."

She didn't voice her evident horror but only exhaled. "Do you think it's wise to go on the road with her in this condition?"

"No real reason to hurry. Tell you what—we'll give her time for your comprehensive cooling-rehydrating measures to revive her. If her BP isn't up to 110 over 80 and her temperature isn't back to the baseline by the time I've finished giving you a crash course on the MSU's new layout, I'm taking her home. She may well stay behind. They surely need her at home as much as anyone we'll serve on the road."

He steered Savannah to the vestibule of the MSU. "C'mon, let's start at the very beginning."

"A very good place to start? I hope you won't set your lecture to music!"

He laughed. This was getting weird. She'd never made him laugh before. There'd been no humor, no light moments between them. Even her answering grin was new, nothing like the steamy, knowing smile that had warped his reason and made him mistrust his senses...

He shook his head. "Setting it all to music might make everything stick in your mind, replace all that data I've made redundant."

"Hmm. A tutorial music CD of the MSU's specs. That would be some teaching tool. I can see it now. *Anatomy: The Sung Seventeenth Edition. Putting the Beat Into Diabetes Control! Rapping Your Way To Your MBA!*"

He laughed again. It was getting even weirder here.

"Will you perform my CD? Can you sing?"

He shrugged. "Haven't you heard? All Latin-American men can sing. Can you?" Just what personal insights had they ever exchanged?

She gave a self-conscious giggle. "Not if I want intact glass around, and not for lack of trying—on my father's part. I think both my voice and piano teachers quit the job in desperation after me."

Poking fun at herself was another thing he hadn't known she could do.

Shift this back to the professional. After their out-of-control scene back there, he needed to keep away from personal territory. They were outside again now, so he could recap everything from the exterior in. He started immediately. "The differences between GAO's schematics and this MSU stems from it being a much more compressible model to allow us to go on some of the very narrow and rough roads up hills and through jungle areas on our way to our target towns and villages. Tell Elvira to hand you our itinerary later.

"The MSU measures thirty-five feet by nine feet when

closed, and eighty by twenty-seven feet when expanded. It also expands vertically, to a final height of ten feet.'' He pointed to the ingenious mechanisms where the trailer expanded. ''I'll teach you how to operate the expansion controls once we're back inside.''

Savannah whistled. ''And here I was worrying about how small it looked, when it will be one and a half times as big as the McCauley mobile units I've studied, and those are the biggest available mobile units. Did you have everything specially made from scratch?''

''The trailer was made to my specs, yes. The towed generator unit, too. Usually mobile medical units have one separate trailer for surgery, X-Ray, lab, IC and so on. Incorporating everything in one unit is more effective and far less costly, but the costs still shot off the charts anyway—which was why I was forced to accept funding without checking its origins.'' Bile rose inside him. She'd been right about him not forgetting in a hurry. But there was nothing to do about it now. Or ever.

He handed her into the entryway at the left side of the trailer. ''We have a stretcher lift here for emergencies. Those panels you ridiculed so much are patient stations when expanded, accommodating up to fifteen patients. Here's the medical gas system and these are the communications system, fiber-optic and copper network for telemedicine functionality, and the nurse call system. That's the nurses' station, with systems monitoring, double-locking narcotics cabinet, medication refrigerator, master alarms, and a radio-CD player for preoperative and recovery.''

''Javier…''

He steered her onwards. ''That's the infrared scrub area, and I can see you were thrown by having its position reversed with the soiled and clean utility rooms. These are really something. The soiled room has ultrasonic cleaner, nitrogen blowgun, instrument sink, pass-through for biohazard storage and pick-up—''

''Javier!''

''What?''

''Richardson Health Group has a busy public service schedule and I did know that GAO was one of our beneficiary organizations. But I had *no* idea this gave them any kind of say over GAO's operations, that their donations came with strings.''

''And now you know, so let's get past this.''

''We'll get past this only if you tell me you believe I had no part in it. I need to know we can work together without anything hanging over us.''

His laugh wasn't born of humor this time. ''Are you for real, Savannah? You think *that* will hang over us? Let me tell you what will—that panting little scene we started our working relationship with. And if I were one to hold grudges, your daddy pulling my project's strings would be nothing compared to the way you laughed in my face when I proposed to you!''

CHAPTER THREE

"I DIDN'T laugh!"

Savannah almost leapt after the denial, wishing she could retrieve it, erase it.

For she had!

Oh, she'd gaped first, her mouth an open portrayal of stunned incredulity. Then, to her everlasting mortification, she *had* laughed.

"You laughed, Savannah." Javier's bored assertion shriveled her with shame and regret all over again. Not that he seemed to feel anything nearly that distressing—or anything at all. "And it's OK. It was a perfectly normal and deserved reaction."

"It isn't OK, Javier, and neither was it normal or deserved. The way I reacted—you never gave me a chance to explain…"

"You didn't need to explain anything, Savannah, not then, not now. My proposal *was* ridiculous, in the heat of…the moment, and I didn't answer your calls afterwards because there was nothing more to talk about. It was never about talking between us."

Talking, signifying something valid and human and meaningful—as opposed to what they'd shared. What had that been in his opinion? Something carnal and base and worthless? Was he twisting the knife?

He probably wasn't. From her behavior with him, he must be convinced the knife wouldn't find anything to hurt. She'd been convinced of that, too. But if all this pain didn't indicate things being shredded inside her, what did it signify?

46

She heaved in a breath, tried again. "I *did* try to talk to you then, and if you'd let me—"

"What would you have said? Would you have accepted my proposal?"

No. It had been out of the question.

He knew it, too. "No, you wouldn't, and if you had it would have just been more awkward. I would have told you to forget I ever offered. As I already said, by then I'd come to my senses, and when I did I had no clue why I'd asked you to marry me. There wasn't one reason to—OK, *one* reason."

Sex.

"But sex never held up an affair, let alone a marriage."

No. But why had the pain endured for so many years? Could sex alone do this to a soul—hollow it out, fill it up with obsessions and stay at the focus of it all? Did sex alone account for all she'd gone through those past three years? All the suffering, all the changes? Was she that shallow? That basic?

Javier was moving away, ending this. "For whatever reasons, you're here, and I've welcomed you as part of this mission. We have nothing to do with the past now. There's nothing to say about the past, and that, Savannah, is that."

Her hand gripped his steel biceps, clung even when he stopped and turned to her, when she cursed herself for building his case against her. "That's *not* that. Not when it ended in anger…"

His lips twisted. "It wasn't anger, just dented pride. I knew the moment the words left my lips how ridiculous my proposal was, but it still stung to have you corroborate my opinion. Must be that Latin chauvinism you talked about. Perhaps I'm not as liberal and progressive as I like to think I am."

And that was really that, huh? Once the sexual haze had lifted, he'd been horrified he'd made the offer and had only been grateful she'd turned him down. She'd never touched any of his vital components, just hit his erogenous zones and ended up scratching his Latin pride. And in under twenty-four hours of seeing him again, she'd managed to do just that again.

But if he'd brought up the way she'd laughed, it must mean it still rankled, no matter what he said. Surely it was still worth a try to talk this through. "But just now, you said—"

"I was just giving you an example of what a man would be likely to hold a grudge about, not saying that I am." Ha. She was still trying to twist whatever he said to suit her purposes, wasn't she? "I'm not holding a grudge, Savannah. Far from it. But I *do* question our ability to work together. That scene back there is testament to that. Sex and work never mix. As for *your* ability to work here, I'm still skeptical, but that has nothing to do with any bitterness I harbor. Believe me, there's none. Last but not least, I question our ability to co-lead a crew who'll be snickering behind our backs—in our faces, too, if Alonso has anything to say about it—after what they've just witnessed. But you're here, you want to stay, so may it turn out for the best."

"If you're sure this is how you feel…"

"It is. Now, if you'll excuse me, since we're staying here for a while, I'll go back to the hospital, check up on a few things. We'll continue our tour when I come back."

Javier turned and strode out of the MSU, leaving her behind, a knot in her gut, a fist in her chest.

A tap on her shoulder brought her spinning round, and she forced back the tears. "Elvira! Hi, there."

Elvira gave her a shrewd look that saw it all and decided on the best course of action. "Would you like me to take you over the rest of the MSU?"

Oh, lord. Did she look in need of such careful treatment? It wasn't a great idea to start this mission looking like the going-to-pieces female that she was at the moment.

Savannah turned on her brightest smile. "That would be

great. Just don't tell anyone I didn't know it all on my own.
And by everyone I mean the men. In the interests of protect-
ing the female brigade's elevated status on this mission, of
course.''

Elvira's sharp-boned features stilled, gauging Savannah's
reaction. Then she laughed. ''My lips are sealed, Dr.
Richardson.''

Savannah breathed. This was better. ''I swear I did my
homework, only to find Javier had changed the syllabus.'' She
told Elvira what had happened, drew more of her chuckles.
''And, hey—it's Savannah. Savvy if you're into nicknames.
Not that that describes me either!''

Elvira laughed again. ''I like you, whether you're a
Savannah or a Savvy or not!''

A tingle of satisfaction ran through Savannah. ''I like you,
too, and I think I'll love working together, working here. This
is nothing like anything I've tried before.''

They walked to the back of the trailer, reentered the compartment where they'd walked in on her and Javier. They
stopped at a row of panels and a platform and Elvira activated
a digital mechanism. Savannah watched in amazement as the
panels whirred open, revealing computers, monitors and a
complete anesthesia suite. The platform became a state-of-the-
art operating table. ''That's as high-tech as anything I've seen
where I've worked. Not that we have the sci-fi unfolding
mechanisms. No space issues in a hospital!''

''The locking-unfolding mechanism isn't only for space issues, but security issues, too.''

''You mean in case of…?'' Attacks. Of course. That had
to be taken into account, considering where their mission
would take them.

''Many mobile units before us were commandeered, dis-
mantled and sold piece by piece. This way, they can't take
anything apart without destroying it, forcing them to either

leave the unit alone, or try to sell it whole, maybe getting caught while they're at it.''

That hadn't even occurred to Savannah. And she'd been so certain she'd taken everything into account!

Savannah sighed. "I see you've left out *our* fate if that happens."

"Oh, they usually take your stuff and let you go."

"But not always."

Elvira's glance was long and telling. "No, not always."

Savannah nodded. That she'd faced. The danger. She'd known about it before coming here. The MSU was out seeking people trapped in dangerous places after all, so stepping into the crossfire was a definite possibility.

Elvira went on. "Once the unit expands, there will be two more OR stations just like that. The vertical expansion will accommodate the mounted ceiling OR lights. The ceilings and walls have the integrated systems as well as the speakers for the com system and CD-radio. Here…" She pointed at dials. "The heating and cooling systems, the ninety-nine per cent HEPA filtration and humidification and dehumidification controls, with temperature ranges from -20 to 120."

Savannah was more impressed by the minute. "That's a replica of the environment of our ORs, and those are the best on the planet. But let me guess some stuff on my own. That's the water system—fresh-water tank, gray and black water tanks. And this has to be the equipment package storage. Is this where we keep the extra OR tables, cautery, crash carts and all the other OR stuff?"

Elvira nodded, her smile widening. "So I didn't need to tell you everything after all."

Afterwards they walked out to the diagnostic compartment with its X-ray and CT machines, then the lab and lastly the preoperative and recovery area where Caridad was sound asleep.

After a moment's pause Elvira tilted her head. "You must

come from a very advanced medical center if this is what you're used to. I'd never seen anything like this before the MSU.''

''I worked in one of the US's largest teaching hospitals during my residency. Then I had a year at Richardson Memorial.''

Elvira's slanted eyes rounded. ''You're one of *those* Richardsons?''

Savannah winced at the expected reaction. The Richardsons were second only to the Kennedys in fame, probably first in infamy, even in this neck of the woods. '''Fraid so!''

Heavy color stained Elvira's dark skin. ''I didn't mean to sound so—so…''

''I understand. Really.'' And she did. Being a Richardson had always been the albatross she'd borne around her neck. She seemed destined to cart it around for the rest of her life!

Elvira regained her composure with admirable ease. ''And that's how you met Javier? When he was in the States, obtaining funding and making instrument deals for the MSU?''

Had she really hoped Elvira wouldn't bring her relationship with Javier up after they'd seen her devouring him and heard her lame explanations? *We go back* and *sort of*, indeed!

Oh, what the hell! Give the woman something to satisfy her curiosity.

''Javier saved me from a bunch of thugs who were out to rape and kill me. Then we…met sometimes while he was in the States, until he left.''

A few minutes later Elvira had left the MSU, leaving Savannah squirming.

She hadn't had to water down her relationship with Javier for Elvira's benefit. A couple of sentences *had* summed it all up. Was it any wonder Javier was all contempt?

But why should he be? So it hadn't been profound. But it had been unstoppable and, to her, unrepeatable. And it had had a touch of destiny, too, that the stranger who'd emerged from the night to save her, to teach her what being a woman was all about, had turned out to be someone she'd see every day for months to come…

Oh, all right. So destiny hadn't had much of a hand there. It had been thanks to her misguided junior resident Jeff that Javier had come to her rescue when he had. Believing Javier likely to be carrying some choice Colombian stash, Jeff had invited Javier to the party from hell, which he'd left in disgust at the same time she had.

After their night-long lovemaking, she'd found out he'd been on a six-month tutoring assignment in her teaching hospital, training surgeons in a revolutionary minimally invasive surgical technique he'd mastered, in exchange for the instruments he'd needed for his MSU project. He'd also been recruiting GAO's help and connections in establishing the project and obtaining Colombian governmental permits for its missions.

They hadn't worked together. And his crammed agenda had limited their time together to an hour per day, an hour spent in frenzied lovemaking before he'd left again, never even spending the night like that first night.

But anything with him had been enough. The passion, the pleasure, the freedom had been so unknown that she'd been intoxicated, delirious—*wild*—and had remained so through it all. After two engagements and a marriage, pointless, passionless and painless to live through and to sever, she'd given up on expectations and on herself, and hadn't been thinking of tomorrow. Or at all. Why think when she'd believed there'd never be more for her, when she hadn't been able to believe she'd even found that much, when everything had had a time limit? Then he'd hit her with a true bolt from the blue: an offer to extend it indefinitely.

No wonder she'd laughed! At the inconceivability of it all. Javier asking *her* to marry him? What could he have seen in her, his antithesis? Soft and indulged and conforming where he was tough and self-made and enterprising?

It had been a total shock. He hadn't once hinted at any future for them. The only plans he'd talked about had been for the MSU; the only thing he'd made clear had been that he had no place in his life for a woman. One objective had filled him, one blaze of commitment had fired his soul: shifting to full-time humanitarian work in his homeland.

Her own life had also been planned out, but *for* her, and it hadn't even occurred to her till then to contest the script. She'd finish her residency, become the next prerequisite Richardson in general surgery, and live out her life a part of the elite Richardson world, unhappily ever after. Period.

So what possible reason had he had? Could her father have been right? Had Javier been out to add social status, connections and old money to his success?

That doubt had never taken hold. She hadn't been able to picture Javier as a social climber. So she'd looked for other explanations, and had found nothing, hadn't been able to conceive how Javier could have thought she would have been any good at being his wife.

But she *had* been good at being his lover. For months after he'd walked away, she'd burned with misery and the need to make him see her point, convince him to return to their former arrangement.

Then finally she'd realized what she'd been doing. She'd been after him to make a case *against* herself, to convince him how useless she'd be to him, how worthless she was. And it had appalled her. It had woken her up.

She'd reached the conclusion that his proposal had been an impulse, as he'd just confirmed, that he'd "come to his senses", as he'd put it. She'd stopped trying to reach him and had mentally agreed with his decision to end things completely.

But it seemed she'd been secretly hoping there'd be another

explanation after all, that she'd retained a hold over some part of him. Well, there wasn't and she hadn't. It had been just a mistake on his part.

And he'd tried to send her away, to save her from the mistake she was making now.

But she was done being saved. And as for this being a mistake, it was up to her to prove it wasn't.

The long walk back to the hospital had only cranked up Javier's tension. He almost ran the remaining distance, eager to enter the hospital, to get sucked up in the expected whirlpool.

He wasn't disappointed. The moment he stepped inside, he was swamped. He welcomed it all as usual, his distraction, his purpose. Cases to admit, patients' families to reassure, results to review, treatment decisions to make, follow-ups to update, permits to authorize. The work never abated. A good thing, since neither did Savannah's hold over him.

In an hour he was finished and at a loss again.

Couldn't he have lingered over it all? Did he have to be so efficient? Now he had a choice between going back to his room to sink in echoes of her scent and presence, or to go back to the MSU and drown in the real thing. And then she might want to talk again, and talking was the last thing he wanted.

Oh, he'd been eloquent, about not holding a grudge and not feeling any bitterness. And he didn't. None. What he'd felt then, what he discovered he still felt now, was nothing as poisonous as that. At least, not towards her. The corrosive condemnation had all been directed at himself, at his own stupidity.

He should have walked away, fled, after that first night, when she'd reached out and dragged the will out of him. The loss of control he'd felt in wallowing in her pleasures should have been a dire warning. He should have realized how much worse it would become with longer exposure.

And he had understood and had done nothing about it. It had been like knowing an incoming train would pulverize him on impact, yet he'd stood there and waited for it.

Where had been his reason, his self-preservation? How had he let unadulterated lust take him over? How had he become obsessed when they'd shared nothing but fleeting, ferocious surrenders to their bodies' demands?

Oh, he knew how. *Exactly* how.

Like any addict, he'd started to look for excuses to rationalize his addiction. He'd told himself that maybe, given time, it would grow beyond physical frenzy, for him, for her. But time had been running out.

So he'd lost his head. That last night, as he'd waited for her in her apartment, he'd manufactured the perfect piece of self-delusion.

Their escalating passion must have been a symptom of something deeper that hadn't had the opportunity to manifest. How could it when they'd had no time to discover, let alone to explore, common ground? Desperate for their intimacies to continue, he'd blinded himself to the fact that common ground simply couldn't, and would never, exist. That even if it did, no amount of common ground would ever be enough to bridge their fundamental differences. He'd twisted it until "more" between them had become logical, workable. Once it had, it had been up to him, the man, to make the proposal of something more.

So he had, and had only gotten the slap that had brought him back to his senses. *Gracias Dios!*

Her reason hadn't been fogged. She'd known "more" had never been an option, had been incredulous he'd contemplated it. Oh, she'd tried to humor him into a continuation of the status quo. Sort of serving his notice until she'd found someone else to fill his…position. He still remembered that smile as she'd tried to coax him back to bed… So he'd let out the Latin pride he'd never thought he'd had, and had walked out.

She'd still sought him out, insistent, hungry, unable to kick her habit.

The temptation to take that last phone call, snatch that last look, had been brutal. But he'd known that one more look would have snared him, derailed him again. He couldn't have afforded that. Not then, not now. His energies hadn't been and weren't his to squander. So many people needed him, depended on him. And then there always was and always would be his sworn mission.

And now she was joining that mission, an enigma in person and purpose, the danger she posed to him was far greater. He'd known how to dodge the blows of craving when he'd had her figured out. Now he didn't know anything any more.

Perfect. Just great. Twenty-four hours back in her influence and he no longer knew what to think or where he was…

"There you are."

Javier closed his eyes. Here it came. Alonso!

He turned on him. *"What?"*

Alonso raised his hands like a boxer blocking punches. "Easy! That 'What?' hit me right between the eyes."

"You're inviting something more solid between the eyes, Alonso."

"Can you blame a man for being within an inch of death by curiosity? We're all dying here, *amigo*. In the interests of keeping this mission alive, you should put us out of our misery, tell us about the 'sort of' the ravishing Dr. Richardson so breathlessly talked about!"

Shutting Alonso up with a punch wasn't an option. Avoiding him was short term at best. Ordering him to shut up was liable to exacerbate his obnoxiousness. That was what he got for having his childhood friend working for him! He couldn't be an effective boss with him. Not enough mystique, no convincing awe—no respect!

"C'mon, Jav! You'll tell me soon, so tell me now. How come you never told me about the 'sort of' you had with her? If the catching up is any indication, it must have been world-shattering. I mean…" Alonso gave a resounding wolf whistle. "Heavy stuff you had going there, *amigo*! Hope there'll be plenty more 'sorts-ofs' during the mission. And here I thought this was going to be grueling and dull!"

Alonso's words twisted in Javier's guts. How tidy and deceptive things could look from the outside! He exhaled. "I see you're bent on making this as upsetting as possible, Alonso. Your insensitivity never ceases to amaze me. You do know you've become an expert at alienating people, especially those who love you, don't you?"

Javier wasn't ready for the twinge of distress that lowered Alonso's eyes. Was he pulling his leg?

Alonso raised hurt eyes again and Javier had no doubt any more. He'd managed to jab him where it hurt.

"I didn't mean to upset you, Javier," Alonso muttered. "I really thought you had good news and I was just eager to hear it. I'm sorry if I've put my foot in it."

"*Por Dios*, don't apologize! Listen, about me and Savannah…" Javier drew in a measured breath, let it out, then went on to describe the main points of their relationship, her attack, their liaison, glossing over what it had been, and how it had ended. "Now she's here to work and will be gone in two months—less. But she's a…demonstrative person and what you witnessed was echoes of the old attraction, the beginning and the end of it all. So just *don't* start dropping lewd hints and innuendoes."

Alonso's eyes looked blacker than ever, serious, agitated. Had he made a botched job of sounding nonchalant?

"*Madre de Dios*, Javier. I'm so sorry—on all counts."

Yeah, he hadn't fooled him. And he'd really rather take jokes over this contrite, wounded look! "Alonso, it's OK, really. You had no idea it would be a sore spot with me. I sure wasn't acting as if having Savannah here is the worst thing that could happen right now."

"Oh, Jav! I don't know what to say. If anyone deserves a break and a good woman's love, it's you, and I thought— Oh, man!"

Alonso gave a helpless shrug, then turned and walked away, his shoulders drooping, the limp of his polio-stunted leg more pronounced.

Hot regret surged inside Javier. *Dios*, what a mess! Could this mission have started off any worse?

He exhaled, started walking back, Alonso's words sinking deeper.

A good woman's love. Yeah, sure. What woman was crazy enough to love him, share him with his obsessions and his chaotic life? Surely not Savannah.

Anyone *but* Savannah.

And "good" woman? Was "good" any way to describe her? No. Nothing so run-of-the-mill.

The first look at her exclusive clothes and jewelry, her neighborhood and penthouse, had told him she inhabited a realm light years from his. Whatever access he'd gotten or wanted into that realm had been temporary and only to be with her.

And to be with her, he'd put up with her people's condescension, disgust and pity. *You do know what you are to her, don't you? Her current sex fix.*

Colleagues had been kinder in intention, but just as brutal in frankness. *Are you out of your mind? Savannah? Do you know who her father is? Or her ex-husband, who's working hard to remove that "ex" from the word?*

But he'd been determined not to be a reverse snob. So he'd looked past her wrappings and at her. It had been even worse when he had.

She was day to his night, pampered to the bone, committed

to nothing. She had only become a doctor because it had been easy for her, because it had been expected—more, demanded. Living for the moment and existing on the surface had been her religion. Yet he'd been unable to take enough, to give enough. Not when she'd been there every day for that precious hour when their worlds had coincided, feverish, writhing under him, weeping in ecstasy. Not when six months had been all he'd have before he spiraled out of her orbit.

When he had, he'd prayed it would end there, that he'd get peace and closure.

He hadn't. He'd struggled to wash her taste from his memory, her touch from his insides. Unable to do it and suffering withdrawal continuously, he'd sought news of her, just to indulge his obsession. He'd found her constantly with her ex, at work, at social functions. And he'd had to admit he *had* been hoping she'd change her mind. *Change*, period. To what end, when nothing would have made a difference to the impossibility of it all, he'd been unable to think.

She'd changed her mind all right—about her ex, her perfect match. Javier had only been her fling on the rebound.

Was she on the rebound again?

Harsh coldness gripped him as he reached the MSU. Then he entered the vestibule and saw her and a soft, warm wave rose through him. He paused against his will, absorbing her exquisiteness and the way she sat beside a sleeping Caridad, reading a Spanish magazine, unconscious grace and sensuality in her every line…

Wait a minute! A *Spanish* magazine? She'd known a dozen Spanish words before. If that. So what was she doing now—looking at the pictures?

She noticed his entry and her jump from her chair followed a more eager leap in her eyes. Everything inside him lurched in response. *Dios!*

Her lilting voice broke over him, hushed and gentle.

"Caridad's vitals are all fine now, so's her temperature. I think she's over this. Before she went back to sleep I asked her if she'd rather go home and she insisted she wouldn't.''

He moved, getting out of range of her maddening scent. "Great! And we still have enough light to reach our first destination.''

"Shall I alert the troops that we're on our way?''

"Being co-leader already?''

"No time like the present.''

"Then go ahead. In which car will you ride?''

"With you, of course!''

His mind emptied. Later, he'd find something he should have said, like a simple "No''. Now the thought of being with her stalled his mind. He wanted her near, jackass that he was. Wanted her near for as long as possible.

Two, three—*four* days, tops. He'd give her that. It couldn't be longer than that. Then she'd run screaming.

All he had to do was survive those days.

Ten minutes later, she was helping him load his Jeep with supplies and camping stuff, filling the trunk and back seats to bursting.

Her heaven-colored eyes smiled at him when he made the mistake of looking her way, an unknown vulnerability tingeing their expression, wounding their beauty. They scalded through him as usual, but there was something else, too. Something he hadn't felt towards her, not since that night he'd defended her, contained her trembling body and nursed her wounds. Tenderness. It swept him, reactivated the fever that lay inside him, ready to leap into a conflagration at her slightest memory.

She wasn't a memory any more. She was a reality. If only for a few days.

Maybe surviving those days wasn't even a possibility.

*   *   *

"You think we can actually get out of Bogotá before night?"

Rhetorical question, Savannah thought. Answered, no doubt, by no!

Colombia's capital was, what she'd seen of it, a maze of contrasts, a city of futuristic architecture, colonial churches and incredible museums side by side with an appalling abundance of waifs, beggars and shanty towns. From her advance readings she'd known all that, had been told she'd be shocked at the amazing mixture of prosperity and poverty, Maseratis and mules, in one of the world's most chaotic, fascinating and aggressive cities.

And shocked she was. More with every meter as they tried to inch their way out of the city. The one thing no one had described enough was the traffic jams.

"We will."

Ah, an answer! She'd almost forgotten she'd asked a question in the first place. And two whole words. An improvement over the monosyllabic answers Javier had been lavishing on her for the past two hours.

"And here I was wondering what you meant when you said we had enough daylight to make it to our destination. I mean, Cundinamarca isn't far from the Bogotá suburbs. But now I know!"

Javier didn't make a sound this time, his stare remaining fixed ahead.

Surely he *could* take his eyes off the road! He hadn't put the Jeep into gear for over fifteen minutes now, and the endless queue of blaring vehicles ahead of them extended as far as she could see.

No answers, no small talk, nothing to do but go back to watching the avalanche of *busetas* on the opposite road, which for some reason was flowing. That got dizzying fast, and she turned her head to the other side, looking across Javier at the extravagant stores and roadside stalls. She'd memorized every item in the shop windows already. The giant-screen TVs, the multitude of mouthwatering bakeries, the amazing collection of tropical plants and fruits and that lilac evening dress... Hmm. Amazing flaring skirt, sheerest organza, and she could swear it was all hand-embroidered. It would be a nice addition to her wardrobe... And it would cost a fortune. She no longer did that.

In five more minutes she'd given up, was back to studying what really interested her—Javier's profile. She wondered which of his ancestors had been a native American shaman and which a Spanish marauder. He was an amalgam of everything these two people had to offer, enhanced in every way...

"What?"

She jumped, nearly banging her head on the Jeep's roof.

Her hand pressed to her chest, trying to curb her ferocious heartbeats. "Why did you explode like that?"

"Why are you watching me like that? If I have something on my nose, just tell me!"

She stared at his scowling face, her shock subsiding and her smile surfacing.

He wiped an angry hand over his face, yanking the rearview mirror round to search his face for the source of her fascination and mirth.

"Bet you won't see it."

"See what, *por Dios*?"

"What fascinates me so much." Her hand crept out to show her meaning, fingers following his dominant bones and skimming his taut, polished skin. "What always fascinated me."

Her hand snagged on his lower lip, glided across the velvet moistness, along the sharp white teeth...

He moved explosively, catching her hand in his, her finger in his teeth, his huge body driving her back against the door. They lay there, upper bodies and eyes mating, breathing each other's breath as his tongue did to her finger what his eyes confessed he wanted to do to her mouth, to the rest of her. Her core wept, remembering, reliving, ready.

With one last compulsive rub against her and a last convulsive suckling of her finger he let her go, sagged back in his seat and threw his head back, his eyelids squeezing shut, his breath shuddering in and out.

She lay where he'd left her, crumpled, quivering, echoing his struggle to come down.

The traffic moved and he grabbed for the steering wheel, put the Jeep in motion and drove on. And on. In silence. Thick and musky and trembling with pent-up craving.

A hypercharged hour later, the suburbs were finally thinning, the roads worsening, their destination nearing.

A makeshift checkpoint came suddenly into sight. Savannah knew it was too dangerous for civilians to attempt crossing those. The various armed groups running rampant in the country were a paranoid lot, and civilians were often suspected of supporting other factions or smuggling weapons or drugs. Local medical personnel were subjected to threats that made it difficult for them to organize medical teams to reach the isolated communities. They could be turned back at checkpoints too. And here was one.

A gunman stepped forward and Javier pulled to a careful stop, his double flasher signaling the rest of the convoy to stop too.

The guerrilla came over to Javier's side, his salute one hard ram on the window with his semi-machine gun. Javier's jaw clenched.

Savannah's hand clutched his thigh, desperate to prevent any rash reaction he might make.

"Don't move, and don't open your mouth. And for God's sake, sit up straight!"

His hiss jerked her up as he wound down his window and blocked the guerrilla's view of her with his massive body.

She heard the smile in his rapid Spanish, no doubt part of a seamless act to win over the man who could ruin everything if he so chose.

In answer, the guerrilla called a few more of his comrades and they all stood laughing and chattering with Javier, ending up patting him on the back and waving them onward.

"So we'll expect those guys among our patients, huh?"

His surprised glance was almost funny.

She turned to him with a smug purr. *"Sí, entendí cada palabra!"*

This time it was his lips that opened wider. Gotcha! It felt so good, surprising him this way. "OK, so I didn't understand *every* word, but enough to know you charmed those thugs and promised them they could have the best medical attention whenever they want as long as we're here."

"Been learning Spanish, huh?"

"It's a lovely language."

"So you also understood that they find *you* lovely?" His growl cut through her pleasure. "You do understand how this can turn ugly?"

He took a violent turn into a horrendous road.

"Oh, for God's sake! We have other women with us and they're all lovely. Caridad is gorgeous!"

"Caridad doesn't have moonbeams for hair." He spat every word out. "And summer skies for eyes!"

Oh. *Oh!*

He reached for her, hauled her half over his hot muscled body. "Caridad doesn't look at a man and teach him how to lose his mind, show him how ecstatic it will be when he does." His hand squeezed her buttock, delved between her thighs. "Caridad doesn't touch a man and turn him into a raving lunatic!"

He pushed her away, an explosive sound of disgust echoing in his chest. "This is never going to work."

Savannah lay plastered to her door where he'd pushed her. As he'd pushed her over the edge of her doubts and reticence.

She had to do this. She had to be with him again.

This *had* to work.

CHAPTER FOUR

"TO WORK, people. We'll set up camp here."

"Here?" Savannah turned to Javier as everyone went about carrying out his orders at once. They were only within sight of Soacha, Cundinamarca, one of the huge slum belts known as *invasiones*. Perched on the edges of big urban centers, they were hellholes lacking in any infrastructure or services, where people were rounded up, isolated and forgotten. Cundinamarca boasted the name of city, if the sprawl of shacks and shanties littering the eroded hillside and harboring almost four hundred thousand people could ever be called that. They were spending the next two weeks working there. "We're not camping in the *invasione* itself? On its outskirts even?"

"No."

"And are you going to elaborate on that *no*?"

"If you think camping there would be safer or more comfortable, think again."

"I think no such thing! I think it would be more convenient for our patients!"

"Camping out here will mean that only those in real need will come to us. It's regrettable, but our time is limited and if we're too convenient, everyone—and I mean *everyone*—will drop by for a check-up."

"And is that a bad thing? Those people haven't seen even a primary care doctor in over five years. In the conditions they live in, they must *all* need a check-up!"

"And that will be the MMU's job: the mobile *medical* unit, which is being readied as we speak. They will provide the primary health care those people need. There are programs being put together for nutritional follow-up, prenatal check-ups, family planning and mother-and-child health care. Others for mental health care, prevention of diseases such as malaria and dengue fever, even ones for improving water and sanitation facilities. *We* are here for surgery."

"You mean we'll ignore medical cases, no matter how serious? We'll just leave them behind for the MMU that, pardon my skepticism, may or may never come?"

His forceful exhalation stressed his exasperation. "Why are you being difficult about this? I thought you'd been told the mission specs. GAO did brief you, didn't they?"

A twinge shot through her. Why did his annoyance shake her so? And just *why* was she so surprised that it did? The only time she'd been exposed to his anger she'd been devastated. And now more than ever, she had every reason to get along, to approach him, to get to know him. To let him get to know her—the new her.

The need to dispel his displeasure melted her tense lips into an appeasing smile. "The last thing I want to be is difficult, Javier. It's just that we're here for people in need and I need to know we'll be flexible, whether they're medical or surgical cases."

His slow nod conceded her well-meant rationale but his tense face said it was still invalid. "Sure, we can take care of medical conditions. But our *advantage* is surgery. This will probably be the only time those people will ever see a surgeon. It has to take precedence. As I said, regrettable, but a must!" His arms folded on his expansive chest, his eyes eloquent with all sorts of frustration. "Now, can we get on with our day?"

She nodded and he turned away. She stopped him. "Javier. Just one more thing." He glared down at the hand on his bare arm, then at her. "That!" she said. "The glaring, the antagonism. You must promise me that will stop."

"Can you promise that your familiarity…" his eyes swept

down from hers, over her every inch, flaring on her breasts, then moving down to make his point, settling on her hand where her fingers lay splayed in frank enjoyment over his hard, smooth flesh "…will stop?"

OK. It was time to come clean, to know where they'd go from here, once and for all. "Do you want it to stop?"

His eyes said everything. His lips contradicted them. "Would I be asking for a promise if I didn't?"

"Why?"

Why?

Javier could have sworn that sunlight had left the day only to get trapped in her hair, in her body, animating her then radiating from her eyes in will-sapping beams.

And she'd asked why.

Don't stand there and gape. Counter her question.

"Why do you think?"

Something flitted through her eyes, another flash of that vulnerability, that diffidence.

Por Dios, what vulnerability and diffidence? The woman was standing there, propositioning him!

"I can't think why you want it—want *me* to stop. What's so bad about letting you see how I feel?"

A stunned laugh ripped out of him. "You don't know?" He shook his head. "What am I saying? Of course you know. And you're playing with fire. *Dios*, Savannah, what do you want from me? Just why are you really here?"

"I told you why, Javier, and I told you the truth. But I *am* happy to be with you again. I can't hide it. I haven't been able to forget you. Do you find that strange? Or shocking? Or is it just embarrassing? Because you've forgotten me?"

I haven't. Not for a second. Damn you!

"But even if you did forget me all these years, you've remembered me now, remembered how I once made you feel, haven't you?"

"You're just—just so—so…" The words disappeared, on

his tongue at least. In his heart they crowded, drowned each other out.

"Plainspoken?" Her hand went to her hair, tucking a glossy lock behind her ear in a self-conscious movement. Self-conscious? Savannah? As she stood there cornering him, forcing a confrontation when he wasn't ready for one? Would he ever be ready? "Or are you looking for a harsher description? Outrageous maybe? Audacious? I'm not really, Javier. I just want to be open to do and say what I feel."

"Yeah, that's a great idea! Going around telling men how you *feel*."

Her eyes became suddenly somber, stopping the words in his throat. "I'm not telling 'men', I'm telling you!"

Yeah, she was, wasn't she? Well, he didn't need to know how she felt. That she reciprocated his craving and had no problem at all acting on it was the last thing he needed to know. He had a rough enough time dealing with how he felt without her revelations, dammit.

"Am I supposed to feel privileged?"

And, damn it, he *did* feel privileged. He was delirious with her focus and desire—she the sum total of male fantasies. But this was what she had to remain, a fantasy...

Her eyes rested on his as if she was reading his mind. Then she shrugged. "It's up to you how you feel. I just want to be honest for a change. I've spent my life saying what I was supposed to say, not what I wanted to say, and I'm just tired of all the shackles and games and pretense."

"Give me a break, Savannah! When have you ever been shackled by proprieties and rules?"

"Ever since I was born."

"I don't remember anything like that!" And he remembered. Oh, how he did.

"You don't remember it, because it wasn't like that with you. But then again—to a great degree it was. You keep saying we didn't talk, and you're right. My shackles were well in place. I couldn't bring myself to say what was on my mind—hell, I didn't *know* what was on my mind, with all the inhibitions and preconditioning and givens, so I kept silent.''

Inhibitions? That had been *inhibited?* And what would talking have been for? She'd told him of her needs in abandoned moans and cries. Hearing them in words would have been too much. It was too much now. ''Well, Savannah, it's better if you keep silent now, too. I told you, sex and work don't mix. And if you're really here to work, you'll leave this alone, leave me alone!''

''Do you want me to?''

''*Maldición*, Savannah, I just finished telling you—''

''That you're concerned for the mission's stability, efficiency and success. As I am.'' She stuffed her hands in her pants pockets, studied her feet. ''You haven't told me what you want, just what you think should happen. They're not the same thing, are they? And who said anything about sex? I just want to be able to smile at you when I feel like it, touch you because it feels good being near you. I don't want to suppress it. It hurts when I do. It's been hurting for a long time now, Javier.''

She had to be inflicting some sort of lasting damage on him.

What she was proposing was overwhelming. Just to be spontaneous with her, to reach out and caress her cheek when he felt the urge, to smile full into her eyes and soak up her answering delight. Now he'd tasted what it was like to share ease and laughter with her, he'd just added to his addiction.

But what about when they caught fire? As they would? As they always did? It didn't take much. They just had to breathe close enough to one another, to think of each other a second longer…

He had one way out of this. Run. But first he had to make sure she wouldn't pursue this, or him, any more.

''Well, welcome to life, Savannah. Life hurts. A novel concept for you, I'm sure. But you have to learn it some time—that, and that you can't just keep reaching out and grabbing anything you fancy. Especially when what you fancy is people. There's more at stake than your pleasure and comfort.''

He turned. But not before he'd seen his words hitting her, putting out her light. He didn't need to see that. He couldn't see it. He had work to do and he needed his stamina, his reserves. She'd almost eaten through them by now.

End this.

His parting shot was the cheapest he could think of. ''Grow up, Savannah.''

An hour later, Savannah stood watching Javier returning from settling security matters with the faction controlling the *invasione*. She'd been grateful he'd disappeared as they'd set up camp. She'd needed the time to stock up stamina for looking him in the eye again. That last confrontation had taken all she'd had. As gambles usually did, leaving you bankrupt and lost and sorry.

The strange thing, though, was that she wasn't sorry, not at all. She'd needed to do that, had needed to tell him something of herself, had needed a moment of total truth. And she had won something: insight into him and how truly different he was.

Any other man would have jumped at her offer, would have at least weakened. And she'd really thought he would, too. She'd known he was different from other men, had already had proof of his dauntlessness, his limitless passion and determination. Back then, though, when it had come to succumbing to temptation, he'd been like the rest. But his reaction to her today was more proof that their affair had been an aberration on his part, as it had been on hers. In his case, it was one he had no intention of repeating…

''That was quick. Well done.'' Javier's voice ended her exhausted reverie. She saw his gaze panning over their camp.

It was made up of fourteen tents nestled against the backdrop of the forest in a clearing about ten miles from Cundinamarca and overlooking it. She'd erected her own tent and had helped with four more, his among them. "And you shouldn't have put up my tent. I owe you one."

"See, people?" Alonso addressed them all from his squatting position at the entrance of his tent. "It worked. He's so indebted now, he'll take down the whole camp in gratitude."

"All but your tent, Alonso." Javier grimaced down at him, then turned to the rest again. "All right, here's the schedule for the rest of the day. I, Miguel, Luis, Esteban and Alonso will go out to alert the local council that we're here, and work out a timetable of examinations for the first four days. Those will be done in the *invasione*'s clinic. I will work out surgery lists with Savannah. Cases will be distributed by level of experience in each needed procedure. We'll also draw up a timetable for using the diagnostic facilities and the ORs, so we can have a steady flow of tests and surgical procedures going. Procedures will proceed the following eight mornings and evenings, with late evenings for post-operative follow-up. The last two days will be for round-up and final check-ups.

Javier turned impassive eyes to her. "Savannah and the other ladies—seek out the *invasione*'s head women, set up ob-gyn and pediatric exams. Your job is much tougher, as there are far more women and children there than men. OK, everyone, security issues. Don't stray alone, ever. Keep your cell phones with you and charged at all times. You as much as see an armed man in the distance, you walk the other way, calling me immediately and telling me exactly where you are. Travel in teams of four, the ladies always with one of our guards, even when together. Sunset in two hours. Be back beside the Jeeps by then. OK, go."

He then turned and strode with the others to his Jeep.

Savannah fell into step with the "ladies", having now met their fourth, Nikki Stadt, a Dutch woman of around her age, another GAO recruit and one of the three international members of the team. She was another blue-eyed blonde, glowing with health and natural beauty. But not a siren who'd bring down ruination on the mission apparently, not in Javier's eyes.

It was too funny really, this image of her as a siren. A siren who couldn't hold a man in her life, who had the one man she'd ever wanted running in the opposite direction.

Savannah leaned against the Jeep and beckoned. He came running. A smile spread through her, chasing away the sick sensations of exhaustion. Those eager brown eyes, that raven-wing hair. She just had to ruffle it, run her fingers through the ebony silk. How beautiful he was. How filthy and undernourished and heart-wrenching.

"What's your name?"

"Juan. And you, *señora*?"

"Savannah."

"You look like an angel, Señora Savannah!"

Her smile widened. At least someone thought she wasn't the devil incarnate, come to wreak havoc and spread debauchery. Still, the boy had only said she *looked* like an angel.

The moment she'd set foot in the *invasione*, a herd of children had formed in her wake, curious, fascinated, tireless. Or at least until they'd gotten bored of following her as she'd rushed around, co-ordinating the efforts of her team, rounding up necessary data, documenting it, talking to relevant people, setting in motion the steps that would set their examination days to a time-effective pace, and doing all that in the allotted time before sunset. As two hours flew by so did most of her followers. Only Juan had stuck with her to the end.

"How old are you, Juan?"

"Ten years and a half, Señora Savannah. And you?"

"Ah, *querido*. The *señoras* don't like that question."

"Why?"

Why, indeed? "Silly reasons, I guess. I'm thirty."

"You're *old*!"

Savannah burst out laughing. *"Gracias!"*

"But you don't look old!"

Oh, well, at least that was something.

The boy stared at her with interest, no doubt trying to figure out if she'd lied about her advanced age. Women of thirty among his people, who lived in conditions of great hardship, looked nothing like her smooth, pampered self. They aged before their time, way beyond their prime.

She stared back at him and saw him through the possibilities of different fates. He would have stood tall, robust and groomed had he been born in ease and safety, nurtured and protected. Or he could have been soft and distorted and malcontented, having been overindulged, overprotected, smothered. As she'd been.

The unfairness of it all twisted rage and futility in her gut. She'd only glimpsed the hot and horrible feelings before when she'd been exposed to sights of human subjugation in the media. Now she was among it for real, the emotions had become brutal. And that was just a foretaste. The full bitter dose would be administered over the coming weeks. Even then it would never be "real" to her, not when she'd for ever be just a spectator.

How many people like Juan had been chased with their families away from the little they possessed and into desperation and constant danger?

There were two million in this country alone, internally displaced people forced from their homes and livelihoods by the armed conflict that had raged for over forty years and had intensified since peace talks between the government and the revolutionary armed forces had broken down a few years back. The continuing civil war targeted society's most vulnerable—subsistence farmers, women, children and ethnic minorities, driving them from their lands when one faction or another coveted them, and making them the targets of assassinations, kidnappings and escalating urban violence. Living in destitution, they suffered even more from communicable diseases and chronic malnutrition. Anyone with serious conditions requiring surgical treatment just endured until the end came. And that was why they were here…

"If you're that old you must be married, *señora*, with children my age!"

Her eyes focused on Juan. Sharp kid. Or maybe he was just echoing the expected fate of women in his society who married at the earliest possible age, then had one kid after another until nature put a stop to reproduction one way or another.

But he was also right about her. Or could have been. If her first engagement at eighteen had panned out, she could have been the mother of a boy or a girl his age.

A shudder went through her. Oh, boy, she was one twisted female if the idea of having a kid was that repulsive.

But, no, it was having Andrew's kid that she found so unimaginable. Or Jordan's. Or Mark's. She'd never thought about having children, but if she were to contemplate it, there was no question really. She'd only ever consider one man's children—the man who'd told her he was unavailable to her no matter what, the man who was walking towards her now with a scowl turning his face awe-inspiring.

She addressed him first, hoping he wouldn't use in front of Juan the tone he'd last left her with. "Ready to go back?"

His eyes fell on Juan and the switch in his expression was dazzling, a kind, interested glance turning his eyes to the molten chocolate she'd adored. "Yes. I see you're finished, too. Introduce me to your new friend?"

"Javier, meet Juan. He thinks I'm old!"

Javier's surprised laugh cracked out of him. "So you think twenty-something is old, huh, Juan? Guess anyone above fifteen is old to kids your age!"

"She's thirty!" Juan's confidential tone and all-knowing

look were hilarious. The subsequent debate of "Is not!" "Is too!" exacerbated her laughter.

Javier turned to her. "You can't be thirty."

"How can I *not* be when I've finished a five-year residency and a year's surgical practice?"

"You jumped grades."

"Just two. I entered pre-med school at sixteen."

"I always thought you were much younger…"

"Any younger and my credentials would have to have been faked. And it just goes to show you really know nothing about me."

Suddenly it was no laughing matter any more. Everything that had happened since she'd set foot in Colombia, every word he'd said, every realization that had been forced on her took its toll, a landslide of despondency almost burying her. To compound her oppression, their surroundings reminded her again of their mission's gravity, probably its pointlessness, too, in the face of such insurmountable odds.

Her smile broke, her breath vanished and the bright sunset turned off.

"What's wrong?"

Javier's exclamation, his anxious step and outstretched arms made her realize that she'd swayed, would have fallen if not for his immovable support.

What's wrong? With her or with the world?

With her, apart from health and wealth—a lot. With the world, as she saw it now—everything. Which made everything she'd ever thought wrong with her and her world seem imagined, hardships invented to counterbalance the excess of luxuries and privileges by someone who'd never know the meaning of the word.

Oh, people argued that psychological and emotional suffering was as real as any other kind of suffering. She'd bet a short stay in Cundinamarca would put that into perspective.

Grow up, Javier had said. It was about time. Starting with erasing all self-pity and self-indulgence and getting on with doing what she'd come here to do.

She pushed out of his hold. "Nothing's wrong. This place is just stuffy, nothing like Bogotá, and I guess I got thirsty and forgot to drink."

He yanked his water flask over his head, came forward again, offering it with one hand, reaching for her with the other. "Here."

She shook her head, stepped back. "I've got my own. I'm on it."

Javier let her go, watched her taking off her backpack, producing her flask and gulping two mouthfuls of water. Then she turned to Juan, pale, still trembling, making a lousy job of looking normal and sounding unaffected. Her pleasure at talking and joking with the boy didn't seem forced, though. It felt genuine, infectious. He stood there, leaning on his Jeep, listening, enthralled. Her grasp of Spanish *was* impressive. The words rolled off her tongue easily, accented, cute and so damn arousing. Anything she did, every breath she took.

But she was tired—and more. What was she feeling, thinking? Was she wondering what she was doing here? Cursing herself for being so stupid? Was it too much for her already? She wasn't made to weather places like this, even temporarily. That damned vulnerability was becoming a part of her and it intensified her impact on him to the point of pain. But it also gave him hope. Hope she'd break soon, leave sooner.

He wanted her gone. He told himself that. He'd told her that. He'd told her not to come near him again. And she was heeding his gruff warnings. She'd pulled out of his arms the moment she'd steadied herself. No lingering this time, no soft glances and touches leaving him flailing, gasping for air and control. He'd put her in her place all right.

Now he squirmed. Oh, it had been easy to play righteous when she'd sought him out. As easy as when he'd walked away from her that first time. Easy as a single crippling blow to the spine. It felt even worse when she'd pulled away just now. Could this be how she'd felt when he'd pushed her away?

What's so bad about showing you how I feel?

Nothing, he wanted to roar. *Show me. Everything. Let me pull you back into my arms, soothe you until that injured look leaves your eyes, stroke you until wildness replaces it…*

"We're all set, Javier!"

Esteban's call jerked him around to find everyone had converged on their convoy of four Jeeps and was ready to go back to the camp.

A wan Savannah went with the women, even when he invited her to ride with him, ignoring his outstretched hand and his concern.

That was what he'd wanted, wasn't it? *El idiota!*

Alonso, Luis and Miguel jumped into his Jeep and called out to him, forcing him to turn and take his place behind the wheel. His heart almost uprooted itself when he found Savannah walking back towards them.

"Got one more place? The ladies have two patients with them that Elvira wants to check right away."

He jumped out, held the door open for her, tried to meet her eyes. She wouldn't let him.

After a few minutes of thick silence, Alonso exclaimed, "Man, that was even worse than I thought. And that's saying too much."

Luis huffed a despondent sigh. "Those areas aren't called the 'misery belt' for no reason, Alonso."

"I just can't believe how close they are to Bogotá!" Alonso's voice rose, giving vent to his shock. "How come no one there knows what it's like here? Or is everyone just looking the other way?"

"Steady, Alonso." Javier soothed him, his eyes fixed on Savannah's grave expression in the rearview mirror. "The horror you're experiencing is natural. You've been briefed about the upheaval displacement causes, but no briefing could have prepared you for witnessing these extremes of despair. But we're here, *amigo*, hopefully the first of many to come, and we'll do all we can to put things right.''

Alonso was only more infuriated. ''The only way to put things right is for those people to return to the lands and homes they've been driven out of. We're just going to be painkillers, placebos, leaving no lasting effect behind.''

''You're wrong, Alonso.'' Savannah's serene assertion hushed Alonso, jerked Javier's eyes to her when he needed them on the dusty, rocky road. ''One of the most important things those people need is hope, the knowledge that they're not forsaken. We may not lift their oppression or cure all their ills, but we will cure a few, and that *is* something. A big thing to them. A lasting thing. Don't start out by doubting our value here, or you'll give them less than your best, what they deserve of you. We can't change it all, but when can we ever? Just remember what you're in control of: your commitment and abilities. These people need those far more than any patient you've ever had. Let's be satisfied with doing the best job we can.''

Savannah could have kicked herself.

She turned on her back on her thin mattress, the hard ground poking into her, adding to the distress of her every screeching muscle. And she'd thought she was fit. Fit enough for a grueling aerobics class, sure, but not for a day out there in real life. She turned on her side and faced the other shapeless wall of her tent and exhaled again.

But why kick herself? Sooner or later someone was bound to do it for her. Javier most likely.

How self-righteous she must have sounded! The guys had fallen silent all the way back to the camp because they could have only sneered at her, or burst out laughing at her naïveté and presumption.

Oh, what the hell! She believed every word she'd said. When faced with a disaster of such magnitude, trying to process it as a lump could lead to insanity or irreversible depression at the very least. It was best to focus on details, on what could be done.

It was also better to sleep now, to recharge for the first day of real work tomorrow...

Suddenly her every hair root prickled. She shot up into a sitting position and listened. Nothing. Just the camp's noises. But this sustained electric charge prodding her—it had to mean something!

She twisted up to her knees and scrambled for her pants. In five seconds she was out of her tent. Their guards were by the fire, deep in conversation, their backs to her.

They didn't hear anything, so maybe... No! She just knew something was wrong. *Alert Javier!*

Two dozen stealthy footsteps carried her to his tent. She didn't call out, just pushed aside the tent's flap and rushed inside.

Everything slowed down as her eyes fell on his naked back, watched him swinging around, his face aggression incarnate, a growl rumbling from his chest, a knife launching from his hand.

Her heart stopped as their eyes clashed, horror leaping in his. His hand jerked at the last second, adjusting the trajectory of the knife. It hit the tent wall just beside her head, went through the tough fabric with one single, sickening ripping sound. Then she was yanked against him and crushed to his flesh.

"*Madre de Dios—madre de Dios*, Savannah!" He pressed her harder, pushing her face into his chest, his lips grinding in her hair, his words a ragged litany of horror. "I could have killed you!"

"I'm sorry…"

She was suddenly free, pushed away from him by the thrust of his rage and shock. "Sorry? *Sorry?* You don't *do* that, Savannah! You don't sneak up on someone like that in our situation. I expected you to be a gunman, I expected a bullet, and was ready to do *anything* in return."

"Just listen—"

"You call out, you make your presence known! *Por Dios*, do you know what I thought in the few seconds as I felt you sneak outside my tent? That a band of mercenaries had slaughtered you all in silence, that I didn't hear your cry for help, that you didn't get the chance to cry out, or even worse—"

"Javier, *listen!*" Her shout stopped his tirade. He stood there, towering over her, breathing hard, sweating in the cold night. "I think something's wrong, not sure what. I was coming to warn you…"

She felt it again, listened for it. His confused look moved away from her, shifting around, concentrating, listening but not hearing anything.

Then it was suddenly unmistakable. They both heard it now. Shouts, far away—but coming nearer. She'd been right. Something was wrong!

In seconds he'd dressed and they were rushing outside, found their three guards on their feet, weapons ready. They saw approaching torches.

"That's not an attack." Javier corroborated her own belief. "They're shouting for help. Esteban, get the van. We'll meet them halfway."

Before he jumped into the van, Javier turned to her. "Expand the MSU and get the OR ready, Savannah. I have a bad feeling we'll be needing it."

CHAPTER FIVE

"How bad is it?"

Javier snatched the oxygen mask Savannah was extending to him, fitted it on their patient's face, his deepening scowl answering her whispered question.

She'd run out to meet him as soon as she'd seen the van kicking up dust in the moonlight, the torches following it in the distance. Now, in the dim light of the campfire and the open MSU, she finally saw their casualty, an unconscious Afro-Colombian man of around fifty.

She jumped back into the MSU, checked the crash cart and the emergency stretcher with Caridad, snapped on gloves, and stood holding another pair for Javier to put on as soon as he came in.

It took only a minute for the practiced team of men to lift their casualty inside, every care taken in transporting the critically injured man.

As soon as the man was secure on the emergency stretcher, Javier swung around to the hovering Alonso. "We need to intubate. No rapid sequence anesthesia since he's already deeply unconscious. Get on it."

Alonso ran to the preoperative area and Javier turned to the rest of them. "Elvira, Miguel, Luis, Nikki, see to the other casualty."

The four rushed to receive that other casualty who was being elevated on the emergency stretcher lift. She was conscious, crying—and pregnant. Savannah didn't get a chance to see anything more as her four colleagues closed in on their patient.

Javier's commands wrenched her focus back to him. "Savannah, assess circulation while I ready CT. Alonso, let's be prepared for the possibility of simultaneous procedures. After you intubate, go ready two anesthesia stations."

Alonso nodded as he finished assembling his laryngoscope, dragged up the crash cart with his intubation instruments on top and positioned himself at their patient's head. "Neck injury?"

Javier exhaled. "Highly probable. We've been as careful as we can since we got him, but with the way he'd been carried here, any cervical injury must have been exacerbated. Collar him after intubation anyway. Go for 9 millimeter cuffed endotracheal tube but don't inflate the cuff too much. Caridad, align the neck for Alonso during intubation."

Savannah's question stopped him again as he turned to the diagnostic stations. "Did you get history of the method of trauma?"

Javier's somber eyes momentarily moved to their patient, then back to her. "Severe blunt head injury. He's been kicked there, over and over, and left for dead."

A cold fist unfurled in Savannah's chest at Javier's grim account. After the shake-up of her incident with him, the confirmation of how real and omnipresent danger and violence were was just another blow to her endurance.

Get busy. See to your patient.

And she did, zooming through the routine of taking the man's blood pressure and hooking him to a pulse oximeter to monitor his pulse and blood oxygen saturations. Alonso finished the intubation and Caridad started positive pressure ventilation with one hundred per cent oxygen now the man was unable to breathe on his own.

With their patient's airway secured and ventilation taken care of, it was the turn of circulation. She announced her circulatory assessment as she started preparing the measures to correct the deficits she'd found. "BP 75 over 50, pulse 70, hypotensive *and* bradycardic."

Lowered blood pressure and heart rate in brain injury were ominous signs. Javier didn't hear her as he readied the CT scanning machine with Emmanuel, their technician. Caridad did and turned to her with a whispered question as Savannah gained peripheral venous access. "Aren't you going to measure intracranial pressure, too?"

Savannah shook her head. "Hypotension is far more serious than a rise in intracranial pressure right now."

Caridad shot her a quickly subdued skeptical look. "I thought the reverse, that intracranial pressure had to be monitored and kept below 20 millimeters Hg."

Savannah injected a 250 cc saline bolus into the venous line in the man's arm, starting blood volume expansion to correct his hypotension. "Decrease of cerebral perfusion pressure—that's the difference between arterial blood pressure and intracranial pressure—is the culprit behind deterioration and long-term poor prognosis. That's why oxygenation and keeping his BP over 90 millimeters Hg are the most important things to guard against compounding secondary brain injuries."

Caridad nodded, absorbing the new information, and followed Savannah's directions to switch saline delivery to a continuous drip. Javier was concluding his preparations and looking across at them. Savannah wasn't ready for the look in his eyes. Was that approval? It was!

Her legs quivered and her heart bobbed up and down with his slow nod. When he spoke he just said, "Caridad, give me BP, pulse and oxygen saturation readings every five minutes. Assess neurological status, Savannah. I'll check on the other patient."

So he *was* entrusting their patient to her judgment!

Savannah watched him rush past her to the other team and jumped back to her task. A twinge of embarrassment shot through her at her eagerness, at feeling the adrenaline pumping in her veins as she watched her measures working, as she glided her hands over the man and translated his reflexes into possible diagnoses and counteractive methods.

It hadn't always been like that. Before that night in the woods, before Javier, she'd been reluctant about the whole medicine thing, just going through the motions. She'd always possessed a natural aptitude for information-gathering and cross-referencing, but had never had any desire to put them to use. Then everything had started to come into focus, and she'd been infused with a new energy and an unknown delight in performing and getting results. At the time she'd thought her spurt of enthusiasm had only been a reaction—to her ordeal, to being near Javier—and that it would fizzle out again in time.

But it hadn't. In fact, the real change in her had occurred after he'd left her. After that time when she'd realized how worthless she'd thought herself, how pointless she'd believed her existence to be. Then she'd come to thrive on every extreme medicine had to offer, feeling alive and of use at last, until her amused and bemused colleagues had bestowed on her the nickname of "Ambulance Chaser Savannah".

She completed her tests and called out her assessment to Javier. "His GCS is five. One-three-one."

Which was very bad news. The GCS, or Glasgow coma scale, quantified the severity of neurological injury. There were four points for eye-opening response, six for best motor responses, and five for best verbal responses. A GCS of 15 was a fully conscious person, while eight down to three indicated a severe head injury and a strong prediction of a poor prognosis.

Javier strode back to them. "Status, Caridad?"

"BP 85 over 60, pulse 80, oxygen saturation 85 per cent."

Javier's huff was eloquent. Things weren't improving enough. "Let's see what's keeping our measures from working properly." Javier pushed the trolley in the CT machine's direction. In seconds he and Emmanuel had placed their patient in the machine, with both Savannah and Caridad making sure his oxygen and fluid supplies weren't interrupted. Once he was harnessed on the gliding table, Emmanuel operated the scanner.

"Head and neck only, Emmanuel." Javier turned to her as they waited for the procedure to begin yielding images for them to review. "So what got three? Motor responses, I hope."

"Yes. He has abnormal flexion." She could see why he hoped for motor responses to have scored the highest. Out of the three parameters in trauma, best motor response was the most accurate prognostic indicator. Three out of six wasn't good, but it was still better than getting a one, no response.

Javier's words reinforced her opinion. "Three is better than one. But that's still not good at all, especially after resuscitation."

"There's also a unilaterally dilated right pupil with ipsilateral third cranial nerve paralysis."

Javier grimaced. "Great! These may be the first signs of impending brain herniation!"

Savannah jerked. She hadn't considered her findings to be anything more than signs of focal injuries in the brain, and not that the brain was swelling and beginning to herniate out of the skull! The consequences of that were catastrophic.

Her own brain felt about to burst with urgency. "Shouldn't we operate immediately to relieve building pressure?"

In answer to her frantic query Javier just rushed to the crash cart.

She followed him, insisted, "That must take precedence over obtaining CTs!"

He handed her a mannitol bag and a 100 mm syringe. "We have to try other methods of ICP reduction first. Give him a mannitol bolus while I hyperventilate him. I didn't want to implement either measure before because of their eventual counterproductive side effects, but we'll use them for a short time, before these develop, only until the CT is over and his ICP is more under control.''

Savannah conceded his rationale. By hyperventilating Torres, they would reduce his blood carbon dioxide content and therefore his brain blood flow and swelling. Mannitol would draw fluids out of his brain tissues by osmosis, also taking down the swelling and reducing the ICP. But both hyperventilation and mannitol reversed their effects on continuation. That was why they had to be administered only as emergency measures and for short periods. Her heart still itched, feeling time ticking past.

Javier was beside her again as he adjusted the rate of oxygen delivery to hyperventilate their patient. Once they'd both finished, he turned those potent eyes on her, reading her doubts and agitation and transmitting his conviction. ''CT isn't a luxury here, Savannah, it's a vital element of the emergency measures. We must have it, especially if we need to operate. If hematomas are collecting in any layer of his brain, we must know exactly where so we'll have as precise an approach as possible to evacuate the blood. Anyway, this is an MSCT, a multiple slice CT, 16 slices per second. The whole thing will take minutes and we owe him the chance to respond to our measures before attempting a craniotomy. If he deteriorates he'll be on table in a heartbeat, so we're not losing time here.''

Savannah nodded, exhaled. Even in the severest blunt head injuries, there was always hope that non-surgical approaches would stabilize the patient. Twenty years ago, immediate opening of the skull to relieve pressure had been the norm. Now it was left as a last resort. And speaking of last resorts...

She swung round to him. ''Why not try hypothermic therapy?''

His look of astonishment made it clear the idea hadn't

crossed his mind. He inclined his head. "Do you have any experience with this method?"

"Not directly, but in Richardson's brain trauma division, it's being hailed as the method that will change the way severe head injuries are treated in the crucial first post-injury hours. After a wide study of about four hundred cases, they came out with the conclusion that lowering the body temperature from 98 to 99 to 87 to 88 for twenty-four hours after patients suffer severe traumatic brain injury leads to less disability and better recovery."

What was that in his eyes now? Something she'd never seen there before. Wonder? No, it couldn't be. Consideration, maybe. Of her information, or of how to tell her not to be ridiculous? Oh, why hadn't she just kept her big mouth shut? Richardson Health Group practiced a kind of medicine Javier had never condoned, profit-based and sensational. He must think this was another fad, another propaganda-garnering procedure.

Suddenly, he called out, "Emmanuel, lower the temperature to 40, and cut off the rest of Señor Torres's clothes. Caridad, measure his temperature periodically along with the other vital signs. Tell me when he reaches 88."

He was doing what she'd suggested!

Her breathing stuttered, then almost choked completely when he turned to her, his eyes intense. "Go put something warm on beneath your scrubs."

He thought she'd get *cold*? Between having him near and Torres's desperate condition, she needed some emergency cooling measures herself.

But just that he cared! "I'll be OK."

"It's going to get very cold, and you look flushed. If you get sick…"

You're going to be more of a liability than you already are. The words concluding his unfinished sentence flashed in her mind. Was she reading his thoughts? Probably. Tonight was her night for extrasensory perception. That had to be what worried him so much. And she'd thought he was worried about *her*!

The thud to reality was nauseating. She'd already given him another demonstration of her "reactive" personality earlier tonight and had almost made him kill her while at it. Less than forty-eight hours in his company and she'd already threatened his project, undermined his image in front of his team, thrown herself at him, and almost landed him with a manslaughter charge.

One thing she hadn't done, though, and that was complain or ask for any special treatment. "If all of you can put up with it, I surely can. I'm probably more qualified to put up with the cold, having been born and bred in Chicago!"

She moved away before he said any more, heard him alerting the rest of the team to the impending drop in temperature and the reason for it. "Cover Señora Torres well, and actively warm her—heated packs to the head, armpits, and groin, and switch to warmed IV fluids, up to 108."

They implemented his directions unquestioningly, none of them giving any indication that they were worried about getting cold themselves.

There was a flare in his eyes when he turned them on her again. She couldn't tell what it was, and wasn't ready for more upheavals at the moment. *Look away.*

She did, a stream of heat and moisture slithering down her back. Maybe she *was* sick. He moved after her, his scent overpowering even in the sterile surroundings. Yeah, she was sick. With wanting him.

And it wasn't just desire any more. She wanted him near for other reasons now. She'd never felt like that, working with anyone else. She counted on his presence and power to make everything seem possible, to provide comfort in the oppressive situation, on his knowledge and experience to complement hers, to support her decisions and give her assurance.

The need to lean into him as they stood watching the CT cross-section images on the computer was overwhelming.

Leave this alone, leave me alone.

His vehement words clanged in her head, drowning the clamor. How could she have forgotten? He despised her, and despised himself more for once losing his mind over her. Once. But never again.

She wrenched her focus back to the moment and on the images in front of her. Her mind raced to process the significance of the opacities in them, pinpointing the exact location of hemorrhage and diffuse tissue swelling. She heard his voice, dark, deep, discussing possibilities and implications, supplied her own views, agreeing with him.

In five more minutes the CT machine whirred to a stop and Emmanuel reversed the gliding table out of the X-ray tube.

"Save and print out, Emmanuel, for follow-up," Javier said. "For the damn follow-up."

Savannah was sure only she had heard that last part, that it hadn't been meant for anyone else's ears. *Not important now. Re-check Torres.*

She did, with Caridad, and in seconds turned to Javier to report Torres's unchanged status in some aspects, his deterioration in others.

Javier stood still for a moment, hands on hips, lips pursed. Then he shook his head. "It's no good. We have to operate."

"Remind me again, just *why* are we operating?"

Javier raised his eyes to Alonso, but had no answer for him. Alonso had a point, and he knew it. But it wasn't the time or place to be supporting his pessimism. He had to get on with his job, see it through.

To the certain and bitter end.

He moved the suction probe to and fro over the subdural hematoma clot. "A bit more irrigation here, Savannah. Gently now."

But Savannah was already doing what needed to be done, gently irrigating in conjunction with his suction to develop a plane between the clot and the pia mater, the brain's innermost covering, to lift the clot away from its surface. By now he knew he didn't need to give her directions. If that first operation they'd done together had shown him she was a superior surgeon in her own right, this one showed him what a flawless, intuitive assistant she made.

This was her first craniotomy. It didn't look like that at all as she complemented and anticipated his moves during every step from scalp division and retraction, to bone perforation and cutting, to epidural hematoma evacuation, to dural tenting and opening. Now they'd reached the most delicate part, the subdural hematoma evacuation, removing the blood clot that had collected between the inner and outer coverings of the brain, then delving deeper into the brain to remove the clots that had formed there.

"Craniotomy has to be the worst emergency surgery in existence."

That was Alonso again. And again Javier could only agree. He hated them with a passion, had specialized in minimally invasive surgery to avoid procedures that necessitated such total breaching of the body. But for the past three years as he'd prepared for this mission, he'd gone back to gain more experience in just about every other surgical subspecialty. He'd done vascular, cardiothoracic, orthopedic, and neurosurgery cases, opened chests and abdomens and backs, even amputated limbs, but somehow opening the skull, exposing the brain, took the cake.

But operating on a car accident—even a hit-and-run victim was something and operating on someone who'd been beaten within a hair's breadth of death was another. Fury and uselessness had pierced him like the drill in Torres's skull. All that rage couldn't be contributing to his healing abilities.

Not that he believed they'd "heal" Torres. With the kind

of injury he'd sustained, the life they'd save wouldn't be worth saving. He wondered what Torres would say, if given the chance to go now and be spared the living hell he had in store.

"What about Torres's wife?"

Savannah's subdued question was the first thing she'd said since they'd started the procedure an hour ago. It startled him, discharged another chain reaction in his chest.

Demonios. Every time he looked at her, heard her voice. Even now, when they were fighting for a man's life. Shouldn't he be distracted? Cold?

Two impossibilities with her near, it seemed.

His gaze swung to the other surgical station where Luis and Elvira were struggling for the woman's life. Killing Torres hadn't been enough for the monsters. Abusing his wife, who'd no doubt tried to defend him, kicking her in her pregnant abdomen, had been their crowning pleasure. "Miguel, status?"

Miguel raised his head, transmitted his own anger. "Those bastards almost split her liver in two, just as you thought. We had to go for a combined surgical and angiographic approach to diagnose and treat the liver lacerations and the injury to the retrohepatic inferior vena cava. We managed to stop the hepatic bleeding by peri-packing and the bleeding from the vena cava by an intravenous stent. We've auto-infused the blood back into her, and she's stabilized. We'll leave her open for now. We'll close her up tomorrow or the day after once we're sure she won't develop abdominal compartment syndrome or bleed again."

Javier's jaw hurt, his nerves tightened, stung. "And the baby?"

Elvira shook her head. "It's amazing, but the baby's totally unharmed. No signs of fetal distress whatsoever. If the mother makes it, so will the baby."

As if *that* was good news.

Work. Try to save that baby's father. What had Savannah said? "Let's be satisfied with doing the best job we can?"

That was impossible, but no other option was available, not now, not ever.

It took all his will to turn off his aggression, to turn all his energies back to his task. There was nothing more to be done about the brain tissue lacerations. Now they'd evacuated all the blood and clots it was time to close the dura mater, the brain's tough outer covering in touch with the skull, and end the procedure.

Savannah suddenly spoke again, her voice thick and husky. "I'm still wondering about Torres's lack of facial injuries."

Yeah, he'd wondered, too. Until he'd been told why. If possible, it made him even angrier. He tried to control his voice as he answered. "His abusers weren't interested in his face, just his head. He was being made an example of. His wife said they forced him to the ground, then each took turns kicking him in his 'hard head'."

Her eyes hardened on an echo of his own rage. They'd never been more beautiful. "I take it he was doing something they'd warned him against? And their message was 'Be hard-headed and we will soften your head for you'?"

"Just about. He was petitioning against their armed control, lobbying for a return to their lands, the farms they'd been forced out of on the Pacific coast. But this was worse than just violent abuse and terrorism."

Savannah's eyes widened, her voice rose. "For God's sake, what *can* be worse?"

"There's always something worse, Savannah. This was a 'hoods in the night' routine. Armed people come into your home in the dead of night. In the blinding flashlights you see only their numbers and guns, and then a hooded person enters and points at you. Then you're either taken away never to be heard from again or, like Torres, punished there and then."

Savannah was silent as they finished the bone flap fixation

and drain placement. Her silence probably meant she couldn't see how this could be worse.

The moment they finished, she let out a breath she seemed to have been holding all along. "So the hoods are insiders? Possibly friends, even relatives?"

"Yes."

"What's in it for the informant?"

"It depends. It could be money or supplies, a promise to give them back something of what they'd lost, but mostly it's a promise to leave them and their families out of any ugliness going on around them."

Savannah's eyes turned black. "And with this kind of suspicion hanging over everyone's heads, they probably back down, killing any reform efforts before they can even start. But I think the worst part is the paranoia and hatred that fearing and suspecting everyone around you produces, turning the miserable community into an even worse hellhole to live in. My God, they're really leaving them with nothing. That's way beyond evil!"

Javier was amazed. She'd grasped the depth of damage those practices caused. Her impassioned response stunned him even more than her earlier one to Alonso as they'd driven back from Cundinamarca.

They fell silent again as they concluded Torres's procedure, approximating the skin over the craniotomy and applying dressings. Alonso terminated his anesthesia and went to terminate Torres's wife's.

As Caridad and Nikki took both their patients to the IC compartment, the rest of them shuffled to the soiled room.

As they took off their surgical garments Javier looked down at Savannah. She was subdued again, pale, her lips blue, her eyes downcast, tearing at his insides even more than the whole ordeal they'd been through.

All he wanted was to crush her to him as he'd done earlier, moan with the relief of having her unharmed in his arms.

He'd been jumpy earlier tonight, aggressive, as he hadn't been in years. Maybe he'd sensed Torres's abuse and had felt the oncoming turmoil? But not as clearly as she had. She'd come running to him with her intuition. *Dios*, if the knife hadn't swerved at the last moment...!

A black wave of horror engulfed him. When it abated, all his reasons for not coming near her were wiped right along with it. He stopped her as she followed the others out, pulled her back into him. Her stiffening body remained inert until they were gone, then he dragged her back to the clean room. He closed the door, turned her around, drove both his hands in her hair and stared down into her eyes.

Yes. They said yes. As they had always had. As they had been doing ever since she'd reappeared in his life, tearing through his rules and restraints. He wanted—too much, too fast, his mind already overtaking his numb body. He was so damn cold, yet he was burning up. That should be impossible, but it wasn't. She was shivering, too. He should get her out of here, take her back to his tent, take her there.

He couldn't move, couldn't bear thinking of the delay.

His thoughts were already taking her lips, drinking her down to her last moan. It would be like in his fantasies, like it used to be. No waiting that first time. He'd probe her, go berserk when he found she was crazy for everything he could do to her. Then he'd be there, filling her, fulfilling her every need, gorging himself with all she gave.

"Javier..."

Her siren call was all he needed. He swept her up, pressed her against the wall, kept her there with his mass and wrapped her around him. He devoured her gasps and she only gasped more, hungrier, getting desperate. He rubbed himself over her, absorbing her shudders, his own intensifying, a jumble of relief and cold and lust rocking him, rocking her.

He was nearing explosion just feeling her and tasting her, his body hurtling towards completion as he felt hers was, too.

He'd satisfy them both quickly now, then do their passion justice later, lavishing all the patience and thoroughness he needed to assuage his vast hunger.

He unwrapped her convulsing thighs from around his waist, put her back on her feet as his fingers became talons, snatching at her clothes. His hand found her, found her breasts, cupped, took, tasted. Her soft cries of urgency were spears of pleasure-pain, joining the hooks she had already sunk into him.

It had been so damned, cripplingly long. How could he have denied them that? Why deny them now? After tonight, he knew work would be all right. And he no longer cared what had brought her here. What did it matter why she was here, or for how long? Why should he even consider what would happen later? Later be damned. She was here, wanting him, crazy for him, now. For now. It should be enough. Why the hell wasn't it?

Don't think. Just feel. Just take and give.

Nothing in his life would be permanent anyway. He couldn't do permanent. She didn't. And even if he could and she did, it would have to be with anyone else but each other. "For now" had to be enough. *Take all the "for now" you can get.*

He drew harder on her nipple. She quaked in his arms as her hands dug a trembling hold in his nape and frost shot through him from the point of contact.

Dios, she was *freezing!* She might be hypothermic. This could be serious. What an unthinking, selfish brute! *Get her out of here.*

He staggered away, struggled to stifle his shrieking senses, shut out her quivering frustration. He escaped the frozen hands that were too shaky to keep him close. In a few frantic movements he'd covered her breasts, adjusted her pants and slipped two more clean scrubs over her.

"Javier…"

"You're freezing. Let me get you out of here." He steered her out of the clean room, huddling around her, offering her all the warmth his body could provide. She burrowed her face into his throat, her cold lips on his pulse point, dragging him back into the abyss. He'd get her back to his tent, warm her, pleasure her and take her, all night, then every night from now on...

"Dr. Sandoval!" Caridad's cry shot through them, snapping them apart. "Señor Torres has flatlined!"

CHAPTER SIX

"I WAS out of line."

Savannah drew her knees tighter below her chin and kept her eyes fixed ahead. The landscape of their surroundings, the intense natural beauty combined with the man-made ugliness faded, Javier's image replacing it in her mind's eye.

She could imagine how he looked now as he delivered his grudging apology. Haughty and majestic, his body language unrepentant, all but saying, "You made me do it."

She could do without this. And what was he doing anyway, apologizing *now*? It had been a week since he'd almost devoured her back in the clean room. A week of silence, withdrawal and averted eyes, more proof he thought it had been another mistake to be regretted and never repeated.

So he thought touching her ranked up there with selling his soul to the devil, and letting her touch him with exposing himself to a terminal disease. Fine. His call. She was damned if she'd sit here and listen to his reluctant peace offering.

She snapped her head up, opened her mouth to say just that, and closed it again. Would her heart ever stop uprooting itself at the sight of him?

She adjusted her chin back on her knees. Damn. Why did he have to be so damned beautiful? So damned—everything!

He crouched on his heels beside her. "Not talking to me?"

She laid her cheek on her knees, looked sideways at him. The afternoon sun struck Prussian blue off his hair, russet from his eyes. She sighed. "That's *your* trick."

His winged eyebrows dipped then he presented her with his profile, staring at the depressing vista that greeted them every day the moment they emerged from their tents.

Another sigh escaped her, exaggerated this time. "There you go again."

His face swung back to her, a twitch playing on his lips. "I talk to you all the time."

"So does my radio. But neither of you is talking *with* me."

The twitch became a smile, if an unwilling one. If he only knew how wonderful his smile made the world, he'd make it part of his humanitarian efforts! If only he smiled at *her*... A pang went through her, more violent than any that had come before it.

She'd known that coming here, doing this would be hard, would probably hurt. She'd known nothing.

But she'd had to come. She had to search for the truth behind his crushing hold on her memories, on her senses and decisions. She had to search for *her* truth, beyond the numbed, purposeless being she'd been before him. The being with no capacity to love or to inspire love.

It had taken only a week with him to show her the truth. A week filled with more appalling, heart-wrenching, depleting and desperate events than she could have imagined, more than she'd imagined she could withstand.

And the truth was that she was no longer blunted. She'd surely found her purpose. She had no idea if time would turn stimulation into laceration, and drive into despondency and deadening. It was too early to tell.

One thing it wasn't too early to know. The truth about her feelings for Javier.

They *had* been all about fierce gratitude and sexual dependence. Talking had been taboo because she'd feared exposing herself, ending her mystique and her hold over him. Because she'd been terrified that would have demystified him, ending his magical influence over her.

She needn't have worried, not concerning him. He'd turned out to be far superior to the dream persona she'd superimposed on his true character.

If she'd come searching for release, for closure, she'd committed a grave miscalculation. She'd never have those. Not now she'd discovered her endless capacity to love, the capacity her love of him filled to overflowing.

It went beyond hard and hurt. Beyond damaging.

She pressed her knees closer, waiting out the racking spasm. *Take it one breath at a time. Until you go away.*

And get this over with. "The line you're here apologizing for crossing—why bring it up after all this time, Javier?"

He blinked his confusion. "I wanted to apologize all day but I was swamped until a few minutes ago. I shouldn't have contradicted you in front of the others like that this morning. I'm sorry."

Ha! So he wasn't even referring to their sizzling-freezing scene. How had she thought he was? After a whole week? That was gone and forgotten, along with all their intimacies.

That night, he'd left her behind and had run out to resuscitate Torres. She'd swayed out after him, cold and burning and wrecked, but had still joined his fight for their patient's life. After Torres had stabilized, they'd walked out into the dawn and she'd turned to him, needing his heat and power more than ever. But he'd just headed to his tent without a word. He'd talked to her again only when it had been strictly necessary and work-related.

Oh, she'd pretended he'd been avoiding her because, like her, he'd hardly been able to breathe with wanting to follow through, because he'd feared the distraction and not giving his all to the mission.

What a piece of elaborate self-delusion. Stupidity and wishful thinking were truly inexhaustible.

He'd only succumbed when she'd taken him by surprise or when he'd been at his most vulnerable, emotionally and physically. Nothing a few moments' clarity couldn't erase!

OK, it was time to stop being stupid.

And had he said sorry for today's incident? He sure didn't look it. And he should.

"So, you think you were wrong to contradict me publicly, or wrong, period?" His eyes wavered. Gotcha.

She pressed her advantage. "Let's not talk bull here, Javier. I gave you my résumé. If you haven't bothered to read it, let me tell you what's on it. I spent the last year of residency in critical care, something I know you didn't do. So I probably have more experience than you in deciding how to treat Señora Inez's post-operative adult respiratory distress syndrome."

"Savannah—"

"And you're *not* sorry you overrode my decision, since we both know you haven't ever considered me as your equal in this mission, and that to you I'm just the nuisance, the excess baggage. So let's dispense with this flimsy excuse for attention to protocol and workplace ethics, OK?"

"Savannah—"

"*And*, since this is your turf where you reign supreme, let me tell you what I'll do. I'll just be an extra pair of hands until this mission is over. Surely I'm at least that, and you can use all the hands you can get. So just be happy you have a pair more. Just put up with me for seven more weeks, pretend I'm not here—hell, just *go on* pretending I'm not here—and everything will be just dandy, OK?"

"*Maldición*, Savannah, will you let me get a word in here?"

"No. And you know what you can do with your so-called apology, Javier!"

"*You* do with it what you want, because you are going to have it."

"How quaint! Undermine me in public, then ask my forgiveness in private!"

"I've already retracted my words publicly, told them to

disregard my directions and to implement yours, and that I was going after you to apologize.''

''You didn't!''

''You think I'm making this up? Just to pretend I'm not so petty I can't admit it when I'm wrong? You think my chauvinism is terminal, don't you? Not that I blame you.'' His mouth twisted as a self-deprecating huff escaped him.

On the outside, she maintained her disbelieving stare. Inside her, everything rioted. *Pull him down, take his lips, wipe that twist off his mouth, draw his gasps of surprise, his groans of arousal—*

Steady!

He laughed again, raised both arms, his muscles an easy expansion of power, his hands rubbing the back of his neck in a self-conscious gesture. ''Ask anyone for corroboration. Alonso will probably give you an exact transcript of what I said. The gist is that I was out of line, and not because I opposed you, but because of the way I did it. It was inexcusable, even had you been wrong—which you weren't. Can you forgive me?''

Her heart had gotten used to being a shriveled fist in her chest. But it kept expanding so fast, so hard, with every hint of warmth, of approval, of resurrected desire, only to collapse again every time he beat her back. That would exhaust its resilience, burst it, sooner or later. She lowered her forehead to her knee. ''Quit changing the rules on me, Javier. I can't take this.''

''Savannah, I don't—''

Her head swung up, her voice rising, breaking. ''Don't keep swinging up and down. Don't start behaving as if I'm *not* just some vice, some excess, some tarnished memory you'd do anything to wipe away, only to push me away and tell me that I *am*, and that I am one of the few superfluous things in this world. Just be consistent, OK?''

Scalding mortification swelled in Javier's chest. Where was

all this coming from? She couldn't believe all this nonsense, could she?

Her filling eyes said she did. *Madre de Dios!* "Savannah, stop it! I never said anything like that! *Superfluous?*" His harsh laugh was painful, incredulous—ashamed. He may not have said those things, but hadn't he thought them? How could he have been so unjust, so cruel? *Dios*—what had he done to her?

"Don't worry, it's not just your opinion. Seems to be a consensus. My father, my exes, even my mother—you know what she… Wait a sec, you *don't* know about my mother. Or anything else about me. And you've made it clear you don't want to. And why should you? Nothing important there."

"Savannah, for God's sake, you're being unreasonable now."

"Yeah, poor little rich girl having a self-pity party. Don't mind me, OK? Get on with your life and just leave me alone. That's what you do best after all, so just go on doing it!"

Could it be? Savannah suffering from self-worth issues, confident, super-charismatic diva that she was? It seemed unbelievable.

And even if she was, *he* couldn't have contributed to them! Or if he had, then it had to be as a last straw, after the important people in her life had done the real damage. The important people and the important *men* in her life…

Don't think of those. Don't! Focus. Think this through. This could be your chance to understand her and her reasons for being here.

Their time together had come right after her divorce. Was this time following another failure, another break-up—with Mark? She *had* been with him all that time and— *Don't think. Push the images from your mind. Just put this right now.*

"It's OK. The last few days, they've been hard on you—"

She cut off his placating words. "Yes, they have, but so

what? They've been the best of my life. So quit that, too. Quit suggesting that I'm hating this, that I'll break. Quit waiting for me to. Enough, Javier!''

Had he done all she was accusing him of?

Yes, he had.

After the Torres crisis, after that flare-up of insanity, he'd run for cover to wait out those four days he'd promised himself to endure, waiting for her to break, hinting in a dozen ways that she soon would.

But she hadn't, when she should have. Those first four interminable days of brutal exertion, hovering danger, sporadic sleep and limited rations should have done her in.

She'd already lost weight and color by the second day and her sustained shock at witnessing the magnitude of humanitarian catastrophe had been glaring. The accumulation of suffering from neglect and desperation was something she couldn't have even imagined. Hell, *he* hadn't been prepared for its brutal impact. And she had almost crumpled on a few occasions, but she'd struggled up to her feet after each stumble and had kept plowing on with the rest, even ahead of them, leading them right alongside him.

Then, during the past three days, the real work had started. The scope of what was needed was far larger than any projections—intimidating, overwhelming. Even he, the most practiced, the most hardened among them all, felt himself starting to buckle under the pressure.

Why hadn't she? Why was she saying this was the best time of her life? He needed a rationalization, something—anything.

The rebound theory didn't hold water. So was she having a purpose-in-life crisis? Yes, that made sense.

Her quest here was becoming clear, her ability to carry it out unquestionable now. And by his skepticism and disapproval he was undermining her morale, her efforts, denying her what she was working so hard for. He had no right to do that, even if he was going crazy being near her.

She was getting up. He always managed to make her walk away in distress. *Stop her, heal her, no matter the cost to yourself.*

He blocked her way, reached for her. His hands met air as she jumped back and started running to the MSU. A dozen meters off, she turned and…smiled? Her solitary dimple was winking at him. His heart fired so hard it must have burned a hole in his ribs. "Hurry up. I want to watch you eating a slice of humble pie before our evening list."

"*This* is our evening list? Which sadist put it together?" Alonso threw the list down in disgust, glaring at Savannah and Javier.

Elvira laughed. "I'll give you three clues. The sadist is huge, sleeps four hours a day, and runs on cosmic energy."

"Thought so!" Alonso's grumbling rose. "At this rate I'll be operating the three anesthesia stations simultaneously for the next ten hours!"

Javier shrugged. "So? One anesthetist, three anesthesia stations. Do your math. It was bound to happen. We've extended our stay in Cundinamarca for another two weeks but we still have over eight hundred surgeries."

Caridad soothed the fuming Alonso. "I'll help."

Alonso rolled his eyes in open ridicule. "*You?* Give me a break!"

Savannah's heat spiked. Alonso was a real nice guy, gregarious, capable and committed. But, boy, was he stupid, too. Maybe a good thump would help his perception. Or maybe it was Caridad who needed the smack. What was she doing, panting over a man who didn't…?

Oh? So we're knocking self-destructive women who languish in unrequited love now?

Yeah, maybe she should be. With herself topping the list.

Still, Caridad's deficient instincts of self-preservation didn't mean Alonso could yank her around like that. That last comment had been plain rude!

Savannah's thoughts stumbled and stopped as Javier uncoiled, got to his feet and went to look down at Alonso. The following moment's total silence shattered with the chill bass of his voice. *Déjà vu* snatched at her heart with its clarity and power. Javier—defending her in the night, in her bleakest moment, vanquishing her attackers.

"Take that back right this second, Alonso."

Alonso started. A sympathetic shiver ran through Savannah. Few things were as frightening as Javier in cold anger. And he was incensed. Any form of abuse to women was a volatile issue with him. His viciousness with her attackers had been a clear indication of that. He'd given her further proof just a few minutes ago when he'd publicly groveled to her in atonement for his minor offense. She'd wished he hadn't gone to such lengths. More reasons to love him weren't a good idea.

"Javier—"

Javier overrode Alonso's choking protest. "Apologize, *now*! And if one more careless, disparaging word comes out of you, I'll give you the chance to finally appreciate Caridad's nursing skills firsthand."

"I didn't mean—"

"Please, Dr. Sandoval, it's all right—"

Javier cut off both Alonso's and Caridad's agitated responses. "I don't care what you meant, Alonso. And, no, Caridad, it isn't all right. This stops now. I'm only sorry I didn't put a stop to it earlier. I hope you forgive me for not stepping in before."

Miguel, Luis and Elvira shifted, tried to walk away, to leave the main players to their scene. Savannah rose, too. She had no wish to sit through another penitence performance. She'd joked about Javier eating humble pie, but she'd squirmed when he had eaten it, and so well. Vengefulness was one vice she didn't have, it seemed.

Javier's calm order stopped their collective movement. "Stay where you are, everybody. As you all heard him delivering the insult, you'll all hear him asking forgiveness for it."

Alonso stumbled to his feet, limped slowly over to Caridad. Savannah's chest tightened with oppression and pent-up tears. Sensations she'd become familiar with since Javier had left her, since she'd seen him again.

I don't want to see this.

Savannah closed her eyes then opened them again, only because she knew Javier would order her to witness the apology as she had the affront.

Alonso *had* been callous with Caridad, over and over. But he was a strange mixture. Cocky and lovable, abrasive and fragile. Sometimes he made Savannah want to kick him, but mostly he had her wanting to hug him, protect him. Seeing him now, face bloodless, lanky body hunched, wounded eyes wavering on Caridad's bent glossy black head…

God! That exposure, that longing… It was unbelievable, but unmistakable. How had she missed it before? How had they all?

Alonso loved Caridad!

"I'm sorry, Caridad. So sorry. It's just I—I…" Caridad's hiccuping sob stifled Alonso's muffled, halting apology altogether.

Enough. Savannah heaved herself up to her feet, clapped her hands. "OK, people. I think we've had enough contrition for one day. For the remainder of our stay in Cundinamarca even. We'll resume our male submission courses when we reach our next destination. How about we get on with our mammoth-sized list?"

"Great idea." Luis jumped down from the emergency stretcher, eager to end the crisis. "I have ten—count 'em, *ten*—assorted adenoidectomy and tonsillectomy cases tonight.''

''*Ten?* And you think you're swamped, huh?'' Elvira rushed to the scrubbing compartment, extra-bright. ''I have four hysterectomies, eight tubal ligations, and two Cesareans!''

Nikki hurried after Elvira. ''At least you get to finish and go. Me, Caridad, Gideon and Alberto stay behind and juggle all the patients you splurged on around the MSU's stations!''

Miguel went to ready his surgical station. ''I'd brag about how my lot beats all of yours. But I won't. Suffering in silence marks a true martyr!''

Savannah forced a laugh at Miguel's joke, and passed Javier on her way to take her turn outside scrubbing. She received an impressive scowl. So he didn't appreciate her interruption of Alonso's chastisement? Tough.

He held her arch gaze and came to her side. He propped his shoulder on the wall and leaned down, his words for her ears only, caressing them. ''It had to be done, Savannah. He was going too far.''

There was no anger now. He was seeking her approval, her validation. Making peace? Admitting her equal status now that he pitied her along with everything else, after that pathetic show she'd put on out there?

Oh, Javier, I can take anything but pity…

She kept her humiliation out of her voice. ''I agree. And your reaction was commendably chivalrous and righteous. But it wasn't the time for it.''

''*Por Dios*, Savannah. This was far worse than what I did this morning. And it has been going on and on. He as good as slapped her!''

''Yes, but before you exacted your punishment we had a not-more-than-usually subdued team member. Now we have two almost useless with agitation. Not very wise, considering our upcoming night.''

His bronze face turned copper. He'd only ever flushed before in extremes of arousal, of ecstasy…

He titled his head backwards, stared at the ceiling. "*Dios*— I'm usually a better team leader than that. But I saw Caridad shriveling and I just couldn't think of anything else."

"Yeah, I know. Caridad can make you tear your own skin off to cover her with. But poor Alonso…"

"Poor Alonso? I may have been wrong to blast him now, but he had it coming, Savannah. I wasn't wrong there."

"It depends on what you consider just punishment, Javier. It was all well and good that you insisted he apologize to Caridad, but for a man with Alonso's self-image—surely you have an idea what that's like? Surely you realize how much of his bravado is to make up for what he considers to be his physical shortcomings? And to have a perfect, superior brute like you threatening to physically overpower him—in front of the beautiful woman that he loves? As you said to him earlier, Javier—do your math!"

"It doesn't add up."

Javier waited for Savannah to look at him, to seek an explanation for his out-of-the-blue remark. He had to make this quick. Alonso had stepped away from their surgery to adjust the depth of anesthesia of Elvira's patient, who'd started coughing around her endotracheal tube. He'd be returning in a few seconds.

It seemed Savannah hadn't heard him. He pressed on. "If Alonso loves Caridad, why is he treating her this way? Can't he see she loves him, too?"

"No, he can't." She didn't remove her eyes from her task, cutting through the last of the grossly inflamed mesentery, the sheath covering the bowels, releasing them then carefully dissecting the intricate network of supplying blood vessels. "Or won't. Take your pick."

"But that doesn't make sense…"

Her widening eyes were all the warning he needed. Alonso was within earshot again.

"This is the worst case of ulcerative colitis I've ever seen." Quick recovery. Good thing *she* had her wits about her today, to stop him making more catastrophic blunders. "I never saw such a severe inflammation of the colon, such widespread ulceration. I thought the woman was cachexic with terminal malignancy when I first saw her."

She paused as Javier ligated the arteries she'd exposed, closing them to stop severe bleeding when they moved to the next step of the surgery, removing the diseased colon.

Savannah handed him another vascular clamp. "I still wasn't sure if her history of severe abdominal pain and weight loss, bloody diarrhea and rectal bleeding pointed to ulcerative colitis, advanced malignancy or Crohn's disease. Until you pointed out that it was ulcerative colitis that had associated problems such as arthritis, hepatitis and skin rashes, all of which she had!"

His heart answered her beaming glance with a thunderclap. Was she giving him credit? Was this how it felt to have her approval? *Focus!* "All that wasn't conclusive until we did the colonoscopy."

"Until *you* did it, you mean—thank God." She gave a little shudder. "I hate those procedures! And thank God on another count, too, since it clinched the ulcerative colitis diagnosis, making surgical treatment a viable option."

"And it wouldn't have been for Crohn's?" That was Nikki, who'd been helping Luis. "Luis had to take some time between surgeries, so can I help?"

Javier welcomed her interruption as he started cutting out the colon after stapling it shut so that the contents wouldn't fall into the peritoneum. "Any help is appreciated, thank you, Nikki. As for your question, it's because Crohn's ulceration and inflammation can involve any segment of the gastrointestinal tract from mouth to anus, while ulcerative colitis affects only the colon. That's why removing the colon removes the disease. In Crohn's, however, if you remove the colon it usually flares up in the remaining small intestine. What usually follows is that we keep on cutting out diseased intestines until there's none left and the patient has to be fed totally intravenously."

Nikki made a choking noise. "How horrible!"

Javier nodded. "It is. At least Señora Olinda here doesn't have it."

"But what she had was bad enough…" Savannah stopped as Javier finished removing the colon and rectum down to the level of the anal muscles, helping him gain a better grip. She sighed as Javier pulled on the ileum, the very end of the small bowel, using about twenty centimeters of it to start forming the J-pouch. "Just living with ulcerative colitis in the absence of any medical attention must have been hell."

Savannah held the intestines away, clearing the surgical field as Javier formed the J-like loop, securely stapled the end of the short limb of the J to the longer one, then opened the area in the middle of the J, communicating the insides of the intestinal segments to form a larger reservoir.

"Nikki, if you're interested, Javier is now forming the J-pouch, which will functionally replace the colon and rectum. Then he will anastomose it—connect it to the anal ring, and, *voilà*, gastrointestinal continuity is restored!"

Nikki's blue eyes widened. "So she won't have an ileostomy?"

Javier looked up, while Savannah stapled for him. "She *should* have a temporary ileostomy that has food residue passing to an ileostomy bag outside the body, allowing the J-pouch to heal. Ideally, six to eight weeks later, she should have a second stage of surgery to close the ileostomy. But we can't afford that luxury, so it has to be a one-stage procedure."

Savannah laughed and the merry sound stabbed him with

arousal, and confusion. "Don't be so pessimistic, Javier. Some people *can* have this operation performed in one stage, and I believe she's one of those."

He finished the anastomoses then leveled his eyes on her, felt the jolt of perpetual chemistry—and anxiety! Her new ease was throwing him into chaos. "We hope she is, you mean. And I'm not pessimistic. *You're* way too optimistic."

She suctioned for him, told Nikki to increase the IV fluid delivery rate, then raised one eyebrow. "And is that a bad thing? If it's not blind optimism, I mean? Why blacken everything more by insisting only the worst possible scenario is *bound* to happen?"

He waited a moment. He needed it to quell his seething frustration at her blitheness. Something had changed out there during their last conversation. As if she'd suddenly lost interest. In him. Had he finally succeeded in driving her away once and for all? If he had, shouldn't he be grateful? So why did he feel like getting up and giving it all up, then?

He watched her turning to the other two, drawing Nikki's chuckles and Alonso's first unforced responses in the last five hours. So she'd ended their exchange, decided he had no answers, huh?

Well, he had answers, more like ravings. She was here on a self-discovery mission, wasn't she? Well, it wouldn't harm her to really see what she was looking at, all around them. To know that the worst possible scenarios she'd dismissed so casually were what *always* came to pass here. Just ask him. Ask Bibiana!

The list went on, and on, with Savannah's brightness maintained all through. By the time they stepped out of the MSU he was at breaking point.

He let her walk ahead of him for a few steps then caught up with her, took her by the arms, turned her around. Feeling her flesh filling his hands blanked his mind. *Get this off your chest!*

"I do think any optimism in our situation is blind, Savannah, at best misguided, maybe even dangerous. Hell, you think saving the Torres's unplanned baby was a stroke of good luck, when it will probably be the final nail in their family's collective coffin. You're congratulating yourself that we managed to keep Torres himself alive, when he'll probably curse us every day of his crippled life, if he can think at all. Without our intervention, his assault would have only taken his family's sole supporter away. But now we've added a bigger burden than anything they've ever known. There's no welfare support system here, no rehabilitation programs that will pick up the shattered pieces we've left behind—"

Savannah interrupted his tirade, her voice a sharp, terrible tremor. "Then what are we doing here in the first place, Javier? Why not leave these people to suffer and die without 'intervention' since death will put them out of their misery?"

Her reasoning was irrefutable. So was his. How could that be? Was he losing his mind? He dragged in a choking breath. "We do what we must, Savannah, but we mustn't feel self-satisfied for a second, must face it when our actions cause more harm than good…"

Revisited grief and a sense of digging in the sea were suffocating him. Then another rabid feeling swelled inside him. He suddenly felt it, the ticking clock. In seven weeks maximum she'd be gone, thinking she'd done her share, passed her tests, leaving him here, alone again. And he wanted to rail against it. Against her!

"You lectured us on doing the best job we can. Well, our best job isn't and will never be good enough. We just do it because it's the only thing we can do!" He laughed, an ugly, bitter laugh. "And why am I saying 'we' and 'our'? There's no 'we' or 'our' here. This isn't your calling or your country or your people. You're just here temporarily, playing at being a philanthropist. You can afford optimism. Then you'll go away."

She stood before him, small, moonlight in her hair, blinding him with her beauty. Her tears welled, then flowed in a steady stream sparkling in the rays, falling off her quivering chin.

He'd hurt her—again! Why? He didn't mean to, he never had.

Oh, never? You never wished she'd hurt as much as she hurt you?

But she never had hurt him, not really, since she'd never touched his heart and soul…

Well, if she hadn't before, she had now. She'd touched him all the way through. But he was doomed to touching her only physically. He'd always known that. So was he looking for other ways of reaching her? Through humiliation and demoralization? That was how he settled with her for not loving him back?

No. No! He wasn't doing that. And he *didn't* love her…

Dios—madre de Dios… He did. He loved her. *Loved* her!

And it *was* new. He'd been obsessed with the wild, sensual creature who'd captured his senses and enslaved his desires. It had been overpowering, blinding, but it had left his mind free from thrall, disapproving, his heart secure and intact.

But after a week with the new her, his mind had been overwhelmed and his heart's isolation breached. Whether she'd changed, or he'd been blind before—or, worse still, she hadn't seen the necessity of showing him more than her bedroom persona before—all that was beside the point now. Now she was the Savannah who could—who *had*—extended her dominion over everything that he was.

But what was the use? She was here to work, to prove herself—and *to* herself. Wanting him had been incidental, just like before, and just as long as circumstances threw them together. Now it seemed she didn't even want him any more. And being near her was fraying his mind and shooting his judgment to hell. This morning he'd committed a serious mistake which could have done their patient irreversible damage.

Then he'd committed another, hurting his childhood friend. Had he hurt her, too, while he'd been at it?

He'd die before he hurt anyone else. Before he hurt her again.

He reached for her, not knowing how to make amends, how to tell her—everything. "Savannah, don't cry, *querida*. I'm so sorry…"

She stumbled back out of his reach, her voice ragged and her words steady. "I may be here for a short while, but I do believe I am making a difference. What you—and everyone who cares—do *does* make a difference, Javier. And logic alone can't predict who'll be a boon in other people's lives and who'll be a curse. I was a wanted baby born into abundance. Ask my mother and she'll tell you I'm why her marriage broke up. Ask my father and he'll tell you I'm his life's burden. The Torres baby may be the ray of hope, the wild card that will turn this nation around one day. Who knows? One thing I do know—if I can't hope for the best, I don't want to live at all!"

CHAPTER SEVEN

"YOU call this being alive?"

Savannah tossed her cool answer over her shoulder even though she felt her eye-hand co-ordination pathways over-heating. "I'm not dead yet, am I?"

"You will be in seconds!" Luis gave a perfect horror-movie laugh near her ear.

"We'll see about that. Where there's life, even at ten per cent life-force levels, there's hope. And you're *not* distracting me, and—and *Voilà*! Next level, extra life—*and* I topped your all-time high score! Yippee!"

"What are you *doing*?" He gaped at her as she snapped the cell phone shut, ending the game. "You owed it to man-kind to see if this game is winnable!"

Savannah's laugh rang out at his lament. "Nah, I owed it to *woman*kind to shut your bragging up! Now, excuse me, I have to run to the ladies, recount the epic of how I beat you."

A hand on her shoulder kept her sitting in her folding chair. "You beat me a long time ago, *querida*."

Whoa! That sudden heat in Luis's black eyes. That caress in his voice. That was a clear come-on. A sucker punch come-on.

She grasped for breath and for a way to handle this, won-dering what had brought this on. Not any signals from her, that was for sure.

So did Luis consider the road clear for him to make ad-vances, since Javier had made no claim in the four weeks they'd spent in Cundinamarca? Was he making them because he fancied her, or just thought her available? Easy? From her

116

behavior with Javier, in the beginning at least, she couldn't blame Luis if he thought so.

The only way to handle this was to put a swift and sure end to the whole thing.

Luis talked first as he bent to take her hand, enveloping it in both of his big ones. "You do know I'm yours for the taking, don't you?"

It was the first she'd known about it. She'd never had a whiff of the fact, not once. How oblivious was she?

She looked at Luis as if for the first time. Striking, big, fit, virile, probably as much as Javier. Just not to her. A gentle tug took her hands back to her lap. "I'm not in the market, Luis. But thanks for the offer. I don't need to tell you most women would kill for it. You know that already."

Self-deprecation chased away a spasm of disappointment on his bronzed face, followed by benign interest, even concern. "Someone back home?"

Was he kidding? "Someone here."

"Javier?"

"Why the stupefaction? Isn't it ridiculously obvious?"

"Not to me. If I'd thought you wanted him, too, I would've never stepped forward."

"Too? Javier doesn't want me!" And she was more certain of that now than ever.

"Oh, yeah, he doesn't 'want' you. He's just falling apart, going crazy for you."

Really? Then she must be even more oblivious than she'd thought, since she'd noticed the opposite.

Since 'affronts and apologies day' three weeks ago, Javier's attitude towards her had changed one hundred and eighty degrees. His disapproval and reluctance had been replaced by every public and private esteem, and recognition of her effectiveness and right to be there. And then there were his warmth and tenderness, bordering on sheer indulgence. In a damned exasperating, agonizing big-brother sort of way! *That* was what she'd noticed, what had driven it home to her that Javier had been cured of any sexual inclinations towards her.

She sighed in resignation. "I really think you're wrong."

Luis's lips twisted. "I'm not. Another man always knows. Not that Javier is any good at hiding it. I wonder why you don't see it. But he must be under the same false impression as I was, that *you're* not interested."

"How could he *not* know when I all but…?" OK, so Luis didn't need to know how she'd thrown herself at Javier.

But…could it be true? Could Javier still want her, at least physically? Was he being all affectionate and wonderful to her, waiting for her to give a new signal that she still wanted his intimacy? She hadn't been giving any lately. She'd been too busy loving him, hurting and feeling sorry for herself.

So did he think she'd changed her mind? It made sense. Knowing his stoic chivalry and considering they'd come light years in their knowledge and understanding of one another, he might consider their new friendship warranted new rules and declarations of intent. This did feel like a new beginning, between two new people. And her intentions *had* changed. In the past she'd been anxious for anything with him. Now she loved him she was desperate for everything.

Not that it seemed a first move was coming her way. He wasn't good at first moves, was he? She'd have to go after him again. Oh, she didn't mind, she had plenty of things *in* mind, too…

"Ahem." Luis's deep amusement interrupted her thoughts. "I'll leave you to your…realizations, go see if the rest are ready to leave."

Suddenly anxious, she jumped up, stopped him. "Luis…?"

"Don't worry about it, Savvy, or about me. I'll live." He winked at her. He no doubt would. Luis would always have women queuing for his favors. "I'm just glad some useful information came out of my abortive proposition. You go get your man."

"You betcha!" She laughed, relieved, returned his teasing wave and sat down again. He was fun!

The moment she hit her chair, her mood plummeted, her elation and escalating hunger fading. Her chest squeezed until she almost cried out. What was that oppressive feeling?

She looked around. The MSU was two hundred meters away from their camp, putting a bit of space between their patients and their living quarters. Nothing seemed out of the ordinary between there and here. Everyone was coming and going, preparing for moving on in a few hours. Her head snapped to the forest. It was a few hundred meters away now they'd moved further from it after the time a jaguar had gotten too interested in Javier's tent. Nothing there either.

So what was it? Her eyes swept around once more, searching for the cause of her foreboding, and saw nothing but their surroundings, which still fascinated her. All these variations within the same place. Tropical weather without the heat but with its spectacular fauna and flora on one side, and barren Cundinamarca with its open sewers on the other. And nothing wrong at the moment on either side.

It must be internal, then, all this anxiety. That figured. Now she thought about it, Luis was probably wrong, had most likely mistaken Javier's new warmth for desire. And there *was* another sobering interpretation for that warmth.

Javier might be complying with her plea for ease and openness between them, probably in compassion for her insecurities and vulnerabilities. A reward for all her efforts to win his approval, too. But he was disregarding the implicit physical side of her proposition.

Stop it. Work with the assumption that Luis isn't wrong.

His vision had to be clearer than hers. Her mind sure wasn't operating at optimum, being exposed to the new Javier. The tender, spontaneous Javier, so different from the blazing lover or the disapproving, hard-hitting professional!

There was one way to find out. By going for it, unafraid

of being beaten back again. And there was no time like the present—since he was rushing towards her.

Her lips spread on the first full smile she'd given him since that first day she'd made him laugh. Since then she'd made him laugh constantly, lapped up every considerate, lovely gesture he lavished on her, but couldn't relax enough to reciprocate the spontaneity. Now she let go, her heart expanding with the freedom of showing him her true self.

His running progress faltered. *Not* the reaction she'd hoped for.

She got up and hurried to meet him halfway on the soft meadow of their camp, imagining how her lips would open on his, her tongue driving between his stubborn lips, one hand fisting in his hair, the other kneading and fondling him, until he pulled her down, took her there in the tall grass…

Those velvet cocoa eyes flared in answering sensual ferocity. Or was he just anxious? Yes, he was!

He gestured for her to hurry after him, then turned and ran back to the MSU. Oh, God, something bad *had* happened! Very bad. She flew after him.

He disappeared around the MSU. Her momentum slowed as she saw the boy standing by its opening. Juan! Coming to say goodbye? The lovely boy had come every day they'd been there, bearing gifts of his latest artwork and *chontaduros*, the plum-sized bright red and yellow fruit of the only palm trees in Cundinamarca. Her heart leapt with pleasure at the sight, then almost burst when he turned. The side of his head was covered in blood.

"Juan!" The boy hurled himself into her arms, smearing her neck and chest with his blood.

Her frantic fingers tried to pry his arms from around her, to see his injury. No! How bad was it? "Where are you hurt? How did you get hurt?" Only rising sobs answered her. Her frantic eyes searched for Javier. He jumped out of the MSU carrying their largest emergency bag, with Alonso and Miguel running in his wake, carrying more. *"Javier!"*

Javier handed his bag to Esteban, turned to her, applied an occlusive dressing to Juan's wound, stemming his bleeding, then almost carried her with the clinging Juan to his Jeep.

Once they screeched away with her still plastered to his side, Juan and all, he enlightened her. "It's Juan's older brother. He's been shot."

One huge wail tore out of Juan, before he collapsed back into his incessant sobbing. Savannah's vision swam. She heard her own choking whisper from afar. "How bad? Why?"

"Bad. The resident guerrilla army was out recruiting."

"Recruiting? But José can't be a day older than fifteen!"

Javier was silent for a minute as he maneuvered the rough descending road with his left hand, his right arm still clamping her and Juan. When he turned his eyes to her, they were full of rage and grief and that tenderness that ate her to the bone. "They take them younger than that. Seems he refused to give up school, to leave his family. Juan threw rocks at them and they shoved him to the ground and he cut his scalp."

"He may have also bumped his head, no telling how hard!"

"He ran all the way here, so we have to assume he's OK. For now. We'll check him later."

They fell silent. What more was there to say?

Suddenly he talked. His voice frightened her, terrible, torn. "This is how Bibiana died."

"Bibiana?"

"My oldest sister."

He'd never told her. "Oh, Javier!" She surged into him, buried her face in his neck. Her arms burned to contain him, to ward off the mutilating memories, but couldn't. She was still holding Juan. The following silence was filled by her snatched sobs, Juan's whimpers and Javier's labored breathing. Javier still tried to soothe her and Juan, his powerful hand trembling over them both. What he must be feeling!

Javier let out a long, shuddering breath then started to talk. "Bibiana was a teacher. She left the relative safety of our home in Neiva to go to Putumayo, one of the southern departments in Colombia, which has been until very recently almost completely ignored by the rest of the country. Hundreds of thousands of displaced people fled there.

"Bibiana believed passionately in bettering the lot of young people through education, especially kids in displaced communities who are recruiting targets of both the guerrillas and paramilitary troops. They don't want education, they want students trained to use firearms. They force 'volunteers' to join their army, mostly teenage kids in conditions of absolute poverty. Usually, the threat of violence and the promise of more money and privileges get them their 'men'. Armed men on all sides terrorize students and assassinate teachers..."

"Those bastards didn't think education was so useless when they ran to us educated types with their every ailment!"

His arms tightened around her. Her whole body convulsed, trying to touch any part of him to absorb his pain and loss and rage. He went on. "Bibiana was working towards an accord declaring schools neutral territories protected from the conflict. She was just one of one hundred and twenty-five assassinated teachers in Putumayo. Three hundred and sixty more have been displaced."

And was he following in his sister's footsteps? In his chosen field?

It was all so clear now—his limitless drive, his unwavering focus. No wonder. And no wonder he'd thought her such a flake.

They stopped in front of San Carlos school, jumped out of their Jeeps, grabbed their gear and raced inside. On their way in, she saw the walls riddled by bulletholes, desks and chairs destroyed and large portions of the school burned to the ground.

Savannah's pain-hazed brain tried to stimulate a response at the sight—more pain, more hatred. There was no more. She'd reached her limit. Now she went numb, moved on autopilot. *Take care of Juan. Get to José. Rant and weep later.*

José was lying in the lap of one of his teachers on the floor, his blood pooled around them. They swooped down on him. Javier reached him first, his fingers going to José's carotid pulse.

He barked, "He's alive. Snap to it, people. Ready blood and blood constituents for transfusion. Everyone take a chore. Expose, determine site and extent of injury, announce your findings."

Miguel snapped open the emergency bags, produced the O-negative blood, the universal blood type indispensable for blind transfusion. They'd collected it from their three crew members who had the type, and from other healthy individuals from Cundinamarca, even a few of the guerillas.

Caridad panted her procedures and findings. "Monitors hooked up. BP 55 over 30. Pulse 190 and thready. He's in deep shock."

Savannah's lips twisted on her report. "Abdominal injuries. I can see three entry wounds. High-caliber bullets, judging by the size of the wounds and laceration of surrounding skin. Close-range, contact firing even, judging by the burn marks. The high-energy transfer from the bullets will mean unpredictable and massive intra-abdominal injuries."

"Nasogastric tube to decompress the stomach before intubation yielded blood. Probable gastric injury. Foley's catheter in, yielding blood, too. Must be urogenital injuries." Alonso snapped his eyes to Caridad. "Keep an eye on urine output to monitor resuscitation efficiency."

Caridad nodded and Javier added to his directions. "I've gained high central venous access and double large bore peripheral access, too. No saline resuscitation. Number one priority is to keep his coagulation up, and saline would dilute his blood and coagulation factors. Start with four units of blood and the packed platelets, pass through the high-flow warmers first. Counteracting his hypothermia is as important. Find an electric outlet and place him on the electric blanket."

After everything had been implemented, Miguel said, "I don't think we have time to transfer him to the MSU, Javier. We have to perform damage control surgery here, get him stabilized and warmed first."

Miguel's verdict in this situation was paramount. Javier gave a sharp nod, and they all burst into action. In minutes they'd arranged desks into a makeshift operating table, had José on it, on top of the electric blanket, with warming devices applied to his head and upper extremities.

They prepped him from the thigh to the neck, leaving his chest exposed in case they needed to perform a thoracotomy to extend their exploration of his injuries.

"Set up the cell saver, Savannah, Javier. It's in the van."

Miguel's barked order sent Savannah's head up. "What about abdominal contamination?"

The cell saver was a machine that recovered blood lost from trauma and during surgery. It spun, washed, filtered and replaced the patient's red blood cells back in the body, providing an endless blood supply and avoiding costly, risky or unavailable transfusions. They'd been using it all through, but she'd never used it in intestinal trauma, when blood was bound to be contaminated by spilled intestinal contents.

Alonso looked across at her. "It's safe. The blood will be auto-transfused after washing, with massive antibiotics on board." As their anesthesiologist he was the most qualified to judge that.

She and Javier ran to the van, pulled out the components of their emergency cell salvage device. They returned to find Alonso had started IV anesthesia, making do with the less sophisticated monitors and ventilatory support equipment they had with them.

"He's deteriorating, people. Hurry!"

Alonso's desperate urging doubled their speed. Miguel performed the first midline incision into José's abdomen, beginning their emergency laparotomy. Javier and Savannah were ready for the critical moment, expecting significant blood loss, prepared to draw the blood into the cell saver.

The blood loss was horrifying. Javier and Savannah struggled to get most of it, and get it back into José, while Miguel entered the abdominal cavity, performed four-quadrant packing with pads to press on all sources of hemorrhage, occluding them. When it didn't work, he had to apply manual compression of the subdiaphragmatic aorta in an attempt to control the bleeding.

"*Madre de Dios*—nothing's working. The boy's injuries—I never saw such widespread damage, such catastrophic bleeding…"

"He's gone."

Alonso's declaration hung in the sounds of desperation and grief filling the room, the harsh, choppy breathing of their team, the heartrending weeping of José's family and friends.

Savannah's eyes reached for Javier's, found a dreadful sheen to their rich depths echoing her streaming tears, reached for his bloody gloved hand with her own, clung. "If we shock him…?"

She knew the answer. Nothing would happen. José was beyond help. He had been from the start. They'd all known it. Yet they'd had to try. Had to add another failure, another futility, another scar.

She'd lectured them about making a difference. Doing the best job. Hoping for the best. Did she really think she had convictions—or answers? Had she thought she was up to this, that she'd grown enough in self and stamina to handle it all? To survive it? Perhaps Javier had been right all along. Perhaps she'd only pass her personal test, reach her limit, then run back to her cocoon of safety and luxury. Without purpose again. Without Javier…

So what? Whatever happened, at least she had choices, and it seemed she was the only one around who did. Choices. The ultimate luxury. The ultimate test.

She took one last look at José's unblemished young face and realized. He hadn't had choices, so he'd made them, real ones, and had paid the ultimate price for them. But he'd taught everyone a lot while he'd done it.

Yes, José, I understand now. And I will go on…

"Going on isn't an option at the moment!"

Javier couldn't believe he was saying this. He couldn't believe he was the one petitioning for taking it easy, stopping to catch a breath. Savannah not only wanted to continue their mission after all that had happened, but she wanted to continue it at once.

"Why not?" Her hands rested on the slight curve of her hips.

She'd slimmed down a lot. It suited her, made her even more arousing. Oh, all right—anything suited her, and aroused him.

He couldn't believe *that* either. They were still in the school, still surrounded by devastation and echoes of desperation and death. Yet all he wanted was to close that classroom door and take her against it.

He exhaled. "The team is exhausted, on all counts. Going directly south all the way to San Vicente del Caguán, without a stop on the way, a few real meals and some uninterrupted sleep, is bound to break them down. The last four weeks have been nothing like they'd expected, and that's saying too much."

She came to stand almost between his thighs, insisted, "But

our schedule is shot to pieces! We have to try and catch up, not take days off!''

Images mushroomed in his head. *Just pull her down, take her lips, her breasts. Settle her down on you. You can still discuss this as she rides you…*

And she wanted to. He'd seen it. She'd hit him between the eyes with it when he'd gone to call her to José's crisis. She'd taken him on a roller-coaster ride inside her fantasies. It had brought him to his knees, inside his own, worshipping her, feasting, sating her and himself.

So what had changed? What had turned her on again? She'd seemed to turn off, to lose interest in him, that same day he'd realized how deeply she was embedded in his heart. Ever since, he'd been telling himself to be grateful for the agony of loving her, to show her all his respect, his admiration, his gratitude, the tender part of his love, and to just bask in her nearness, the only thing he'd have of her.

Then she'd suddenly turned on again. Or had she been turned on, period? Had this explicit invitation been for *him*, or had she just been hungry, frustrated? Had that scene with Luis had anything to do with her state?

Dios, was this how men had heart attacks?

Jealousy. He'd thought he'd known it before, imagining Savannah with Mark, with other men, since he'd walked out of her life. Acrid, warping, destructive. Preying on his stamina and sanity.

He'd known nothing.

But he had no claim on her and jealousy wasn't his right, or his luxury. Yet—what if she wanted him again? Would he take what he could? Four weeks with her. He no longer simply wanted or craved her. He was suffocating for her. It was no longer sustenance to have her, it was survival.

Didn't it follow that walking away from her would be fatal this time?

''Hel-lo! Javier? Did you get that last part?''

"Of course, I did!" How could he not, when his focus on her was total? "And I hope we won't fight over this decision, Savannah. Let me have this say uncontested. It's for the best, for everyone."

"A rest is all well and good, but we should have been to San Vicente del Caguán and gone by now. Going any more off course…"

"We won't be off course. Stopping at Neiva is right on our way. Tell you what—if, after a couple of days, everyone is up to moving on again, we'll set out. There's no use having an overworked, overwrought team on the road, Savannah. You know we'd be liable to cause more harm than good that way."

Her heavenly eyes fixed him, filling with—what? Would he ever figure her out? Her sigh of agreement emptied his own lungs. "All right. Oh, you're right. Of course you are. I'm just— I don't…" It was clear what filled her eyes now. Tears. Would they ever hurt him any less? "I—I wanted to get busy, move on, be of use. Resting, you get to think, to dwell on stuff…"

Four weeks ago he would have never believed this day would come, that Savannah would stand there, sharing his drive, echoing his objectives, seeking solace through work, through service. He couldn't afford to dwell on that now. Couldn't afford to love her any deeper!

But he could give her comfort. He knew just how, every lick and caress and stroke as he took her, from herself and into delirium, into ecstasy…

He watched her eyes clearing, filling with answering awareness, then suddenly with realization, excitement. "We'll be stopping in Neiva? Your hometown? Oh, Javier, will you stay with your family? Will you take me to visit them?"

Take her to his family home? Show her once and for all exactly why she should never give him any serious consideration?

He shook his head. "I've already phoned ahead and booked you all into one of the city's better hotels."

"So! You'd already taken the decision to go to Neiva and carried it out, notwithstanding your co-leader's opinion!"

That wasn't irritation—she was bordering on humor as far as she could in their current mood and situation. But it seemed it had distracted her from the family visit issue. Relief boosted his own mood a bit. "*Sí*, I took matters into my own hands. Are you going to punish me?"

She bent and pushed her face closer to his, gave him a magnified view of her beauty. Like that first day, when her antics had taken him by storm, forced his laughter and started rewriting her character in his mind. "You bet. And you won't even know how or when. You'll just live on, sweating it!"

Look away. You've got no fight left. You're half a breath away from total insanity.

Looking away only took his drugged gaze from her eyes to her breasts.

Her voice was husky. "So you got accommodation sorted out. What does that have to do with visiting your family? I would still like to meet them, Javier. I'd love to see your home."

Had he vapor-locked, like an overheated engine? All the symptoms were there. Nothing was working and everything inside him was boiling over. Forming words, producing sound was agony now. "We'll see!"

"As in, drop the subject until it's forgotten? As in, get it through your head, I'm not inviting you to my home?"

There was mockery in her voice but it was the tinge of hurt that had him dragging burning eyes to hers and got his voice working. "I didn't mean that…"

"Then invite me, Javier."

What the hell! Invite her and let her see your life as it is and as you've chosen to live it. It isn't as if she'd think of sharing it anyway. Just give her your invitation—your sur-render, like that first night...

"Dr. Sandoval? They need you to sign the...the death cer-tificate."

Caridad. For the second time pulling him back from the precipice.

This time he didn't want to step back. He craved the over-powering sweetness, the liberation of jumping to his doom.

CHAPTER EIGHT

"IT WASN'T all doom and gloom, y'know!"

Savannah heard herself giggling the words.

Oh, lord! She was having a breakdown! Could she sound more giddy and silly and frivolous?

Not that her audience thought so. The eyes locked on her flashed "pretentious", "thoughtless", "irritating" in ten-foot-high neon letters. And that was for starters.

Stop talking. Breathe. You don't have to win anyone's approval. You're doing a rotten job of it anyway.

Oh, why was she here? Why had she insisted Javier take her to visit his family? Why couldn't she stop talking? Why had she ever learned Spanish?

"Do you know how many operations we did?" she heard herself informing her clearly numbed listeners. "In twenty-eight days we totaled two thousand eight hundred fifty-six cases, over a hundred cases a day. And all of them followed up, too. I'd say that's some achievement, even if Javier likes to look on the dark side—the patients we couldn't help, I mean!"

Help! Somebody stop her. Oh, why wasn't anyone saying anything?

They hadn't said anything at all since they'd introduced themselves to her outside Javier's tiny family hacienda. Afterwards, they'd just followed her and Javier inside to the small reception area and now sat, a grossly over-packed, silent audience, witnessing her make a fool of herself.

She just hadn't thought there'd be so *many* of them!

Javier had said he had seven brothers and sisters. It turned out that was not counting Bibiana. And then there were his

131

parents, his grandparents, on both sides, the in-laws, his aunts and uncles, his cousins, not to mention the *children*! All in all there were over a hundred of them. She'd stopped registering names after the first three dozen, had forgotten the ones she had registered.

His younger brother—Tadeo, or was he Severo?—had said they were gathered in full force like that for occasions only, birthdays, fiestas, funerals. Javier's return after over a year away warranted the assembly. Just her luck!

Tadeo—or Severo—mercifully put an end to her prattling. "That *is* a great achievement. And we all know Javier is one of the world's leading perfectionist-idealist-pessimists."

Javier bowed his head nonchalantly, without taking his eyes off her. Was it any wonder she was on the edge of hysterical laughter? It was Javier's focus, not the group's, that was shorting out her restraint circuits. Not that the latter was helping. "My gloomy outlook aside, I've been telling Savannah we had to stop the mission to rest and get some real meals. Any to be had around here, *madre*?"

Javier's teasing seemed to snap the invisible muffler that had been keeping the crowd, even the children and babies, silent. What followed was mayhem. An avalanche of chatting, laughter, questions, shrieks, yells erupted, then escalated, and was sustained all through the seemingly endless preparations of the banquet-like lunch-cum-dinner.

Savannah tried to offer her help and was only shoved around by the sheer pressure of the masses, until she gave up. Five hours later, every level surface in the house had dozens of service dishes filled with the same food. Everyone spread everywhere, the cacophony intensifying as eating started. She was swept with the flow of people going to sit down in the dining room, where the twelve-seater table now had makeshift extensions, seating forty-something people, almost on each other's laps.

Her first real look at Colombian cuisine was a revelation. And more than a slight shock.

"That's *sancocho*, one of our national dishes." Javier's mother put her lips to Savannah's ear to counteract the clamor, her harsh voice extra loud in compensation, making Savannah jump. "It's stewed rooster."

"Feet and all, huh?" Savannah almost tasted her own foot. And the woman had *finally* addressed her, though very stiltedly and only because of Javier's repeated subtle prodding. She only hoped her foot would keep her mouth shut until Javier got her out of there.

To Señora Alejandra's credit, she didn't bat an eyelid at Savannah's crack. "Don't try them if you're wary. They won't go to waste with all the mouths around here."

Savannah's words stumbled over each other in her haste to make amends. "Oh, I'm not wary and everything smells mouthwatering. I was just wondering at all that colorful stuff served with it!"

Señora Alejandra was the feminine equivalent of her son, and the slashed features and dominant bones didn't flatter her. Not to mention that her hard life was detailed in every embittered, grieving line of her weathered face. Her attempted smile didn't come off well. "That's avocado salad, steamed saffron rice and the small baked dough cakes are called *arepa*."

"And what's that there?" Savannah had her suspicions, but just couldn't credit them. Surely it couldn't be...

"Ants." One of Javier's sisters, the willowy one—Alba?—answered her, her gleaming brown eyes roving from Savannah's eyes to her hair to her creamy exposed arms. "That's another thing you can avoid."

Don't you dare gag! Savannah forced a too bright smile as she reached for one. "I love trying new food!"

Tadeo—definitely Tadeo—guffawed as she put one in her mouth. "Stop! You only eat the crunchy abdomen!"

Now he tells her. And did he have to say *abdomen*? Savannah's stomach heaved. She carefully got the ant out of her mouth, and another of Javier's sisters, the earth-mother one—Carmela?—enlightened her. "These are specially raised *Hormigas Culonas* which have enlarged abdomens. They're cleaned then roasted or fried and served with cheese or honey. Just dip the abdomen in honey and bite it off. They're sort of like partially popped kernels of corn."

And they were. After she'd gotten her stomach under control Savannah threw herself into the experience, and enjoyed it. A lot.

"Hey, this could be as addictive as popcorn!" Savannah licked her fingers clean of honey, eagerly reaching for yet another ant—and met Javier's eyes. His devouring eyes. His lids lowered, raising her gaze's temperature and hers, melting down to her lips, following her tongue's movements, his own sweeping his upper lip, dragging out memories of it on her, in her. Then his teeth sank into his lower lip. She jerked, feeling them sinking into her, right down to her soul.

Ever since they'd been at San Carlos school, then all the way to Neiva, back beside him in his Jeep, blind to the magnificent tropical scenery on the way, going crazy wanting her hands and lips all over him, she'd still had doubts. His intensity could have been some other form of passion, a residue of their wrenching crisis.

No doubt any more. Luis had been right. Javier still wanted her.

So why was he still holding back? His early worries no longer existed. Work wouldn't be affected. Neither would their effectiveness as team leaders. He should know that by now. Maybe he was confused over her on-off behavior?

That was easy to fix. Just give her a couple of hours alone with him, a locked room, a bed, and she'd put him straight.

But…if confusion wasn't the reason, one explanation was left. He didn't want to start something empty and temporary again. And was that what she had to be in his opinion—even now he seemed to think the world of her? Empty and temporary had been all she'd been good for *then*. This was *now*.

And are you sure "now" is so different?

Yes, she was. Positive. She now knew who she was. And so should he. Why was his mind unchanged?

Put that way, only one answer was available. No matter how much had changed, *his* feelings for her remained empty and temporary. Did his honor and their new friendship dictate against getting sexually involved with her again, knowing that? It seemed so.

So one thing hadn't changed about her: her ability to inspire love.

Fine. That wasn't stopping her this time. He wanted her now, for now, and that had to be enough. The alternative of being without him was no alternative at all.

"Are you all right?" That was Tadeo, reaching out to push the ant plate out of her reach. "You went crimson all of a sudden. Maybe you shouldn't eat so many ants your first time. Maybe your tongue and stomach agree but your mind doesn't."

"Oh, I'm fine." She didn't object to the dish's removal, though, could barely drag her eyes away from Javier.

"This will be something more to your liking, I hope." Señora Alejandra tapped her hand, alerting her to the arrival of fruit.

At any other time Savannah would have drooled at the sight of papayas the size of watermelons, mangoes that had to weigh two pounds each and coconuts that looked like they contained three glasses of coconut milk. Right now, as she looked at Javier, she only wanted to eat him.

A booming voice right in her ear and the tantalizing, powerful aroma of coffee dampened her arousal from a cramping agony to a pervasive ache.

"Would you like some *tinto*?"

She snapped her head around, found Javier's father standing behind her chair. "Huh?"

"That's strong black Colombian coffee, considered the richest in the world. It will wake anyone from their deepest slumber with a smile."

She knew what would wake her up with a smile. Javier's hands on her, sparking her circuits, his breath on her frying them, his weight all over her grounding her before she burned out. For now she took the coffee.

In a couple more hours it was midnight and the mood of the gathering heightened, giving her a heart-melting view of Javier, outgoing, totally at ease, bantering and guffawing with her and with his family. The hilarity of the crowd grew to hysterical proportions when the male cousins started ribbing each other with embarrassing revelations. Javier had the most damaging information on everyone, and to his contemporaries' chagrin, they had nothing of similar relevance on him.

"Javier the infallible." One of his cousins, the one even bigger than Esteban, smirked. "Wonder why we put up with you all these years!"

Javier smirked right back, macho feathers preened. "Maybe because you needed someone to pull you out of jams in one piece?"

"Watch it, *hermano pequeño*!" His older brother, Severo, pushed his face into Javier's. "No little brother of mine ever pulled me out of anything."

"*Sí?* How about that time when I had to rush all the way to Cali to save you from—shall we say, an amorous mishap? I got to that house just in—"

Severo choked, everyone burst out laughing at his wife's thunderous expression and Javier stopped and amended, "You were twenty-five then, long before you met Hermana."

Tadeo gave him a considering look. "You know, Javier, we can truss you up to shut you up. We've done it before."

"You can try. I was out of your amateur restraints in minutes."

Another cousin warned, "I'm into shipping crates now, Jav. My knots won't be so amateurish now."

Javier tossed him a taunting look. "I seem to remember a very interesting time, Domingo, when you were trying to fix your car..."

Domingo jumped up. "That's it. Get him, guys!"

For the next few minutes there was chaos—shouts and guffaws as a dozen big men jumped Javier, held him down and tied him up. Savannah watched, openmouthed and burning with envy. What she wouldn't give to have the same freedom with him! Then they carried him off to his house a few blocks away, howling with laughter. They'd see how long it would take him to get out of his restraints this time.

Suddenly, a white-hot idea zapped through her.

Javier, alone, in his house, on his bed, unable to get up, and there for as long as she needed to get their situation sorted out.

That was an opportunity to kill for!

"You do know I'll kill you all, don't you?"

Raucous, receding laughter answered Javier's shouted threat. Those man-sized rats knew he had to get out of his bonds first to carry it out. Which, it seemed, he wouldn't. Domingo hadn't been bragging about the improvement in his knot-tying know-how.

Slow down. Think. They'll come back. Then again, probably not for a few hours. Maybe not tonight.

OK. So he'd pushed it. He'd been out of control, elated, intoxicated—insanely frustrated, sitting there, watching Savannah being tossed about by the waves of his family's irrepressible momentum, but still chattering, joining in—eating ants, *por Dios*! He'd wanted to drag her over the table and take her right on top of it, there and then...

Come down. Focus. He had to get out of those ropes, to get back to her, to take her back to her hotel. Those idiots hadn't thought of that, had they?

He struggled with his restraints once more, his aggravation mounting.

Stop it. Pulling on the knots would only tighten them. Slowly but surely…surely— Someone was in the house!

Coming back to untie him? Who would it be? And how much would he have to grovel before they did?

His small bedroom felt suddenly smaller in the pitch dark. There hadn't been a sound again, or a scent yet, but he knew. Savannah. It was her out there!

A light flicked on outside, an uneven two-inch beam under the shoddy door. The next second, the imperfect mechanism of the door handle cracked open, the sound as loud as a bullet in the silence. Her figure flowed forward, framed in the wedge of light, a white-fire-rimmed silhouette.

His breath wouldn't come, his heart wouldn't beat. Silent steps brought her into the room. Her scent hit him then, followed by her siren call.

"Javier…"

His heart beat now, choking him with erratic thumps.

Don't you dare pass out! Say something.

"So my father—gave you—the key, too?" *Dios!* Could he sound more worked up?

"No, I worked on Tadeo…" He couldn't see her face, but her voice was hot honey pouring onto his overextended senses. "He got me here, let me in."

That figured. By now, Tadeo would probably only ask how high if she said jump. He'd been bowled over, as every other man in the house had been. The women had been envious, though they hadn't disgraced him. But *everyone* had dropped a word here or there. The same curiosity, same incredulity. What was this vision doing here? In Colombia? With the MSU? With him?

He'd had no answers, since everything he believed was only conjecture. And she wasn't *with* him.

But now she was.

She came closer, and he sensed it, scented it—her hunger. His every muscle clenched, vibrated with tension, like that first night, when she'd reached for him and he'd tried to resist, to be noble, to be sane.

"OK, I give up." Someone else's voice, disjointed and disturbed, issued from him. "I can't undo my restraints…" Not in his disintegrating state. "Help me?"

"Uh, I don't think so." The mischievous smile in her voice lit up the room, and his heart. "I kinda like you like that."

"Savannah…"

"Yes, say my name like that. I've missed that so much. Oh, God—so much!" Her voice sank lower, and so did she beside him on the bed.

He found himself obeying her, gasping her name again, then again.

One hand went to his chest, rested on his booming heart. He would have jerked off the bed if he hadn't been spread-eagled and tethered.

He couldn't survive this. "Savannah, *por favor*—just undo my right hand. I'll take care of the rest…"

Her answer was to bend across him. To reach his right hand? *Dios*, no—to rest her cheek on his chest. She just lay there for a moment, breathing deeply, each shuddering breath shaking him apart. Then she turned her lips to him, and started undoing his buttons with her teeth, teeth that sank into his muscles, over his heart, in the most delicate devouring. Had he thought it too much moments ago? Was she out to kill him?

Her shudders grew as she pressed her whole face against his chest. The heart she'd already sucked dry bashed itself against his ribs, the barrier between it and a direct taste of her kiss.

It was over. He'd never fight again. He'd been hers from that first night. She was just renewing her claim, her ownership.

She slithered up his body, her breasts flattening against him, the sweep of her thigh against his engorged flesh causing an arousal that left him grunting for breath. Her journey up his body ended with her face nuzzling his. He gasped for her lips. They just skimmed his, his nose, his febrile eyes and knotted brow, ending where it had all started—at his forehead.

His head snapped back from the brand she'd burnt into his skin. He arched back, like a drowning man resurfacing. She followed, her teeth at his pulse point, drawing the life out of him. "Javier, darling, don't hold back any more, don't think of what next. Don't think at all."

Don't think of what next. Why? Because there'd be no *what next*?

Just take now! "Savannah—*por Dios, misericordia.* Have mercy—let me up…"

"So you can walk away from me again? Do you realize how many times you've done that, Javier?"

· Not once. That hadn't been walking out or walking away. That had been running for his life. He could no longer run. Even without the fetters, she had him wherever and however and as long as she wanted him. He closed his eyes tight and waited for her to take him into whatever dimension she pleased.

A sudden chill tore through him. *She's moving away*, his body screamed.

Settle down! She had to be taking her clothes off, then it would be his turn, then she would take him, bury him inside her, feed her hunger and drain him of every need and tension and worry…

The chill intensified and his eyes snapped open. She wasn't undressing but just sitting there, rigid, breathing hard. Then she was getting up.

But he'd surrendered!

"Savannah!"

"You don't want this, do you? And I've been— Oh, God! This is as good as forcing you. Oh, hell, Javier—I'm so sorry…"

"*¿Estás loca?*" His laugh was frenzied at the insanity of her words. "Not want you? You're crazy, right?"

"You mean…you do want me? Oh, darling… Then just take me—take me back!"

"How can I when I'm tied up like this?"

Her agitation dissipated. He could almost see it in the murky shadows, spiraling out of her. Then the vibrant mischief and desire started to emanate from her again.

"Free me, Savannah. *¡Por el amor de Dios.* Untie me…"

"Uh-uh." Her lips landed in his abdomen this time, her tongue in his navel. He roared.

"Savannah—if you don't mean to kill me, let me touch you!"

"Later, darling. It's my turn now. You think I'm letting this opportunity pass? All of you, every magnificent muscle and sinew and shudder at my disposal?" Her hands and lips and teeth were everywhere now his shirt was halfway down his bunched arms. "I'm making up for three years and one month, taking every inch and groan and liberty I've been going crazy for. Let me enjoy you, let me pleasure you."

Her ragged words twisted inside him, an aphrodisiac overdose. "At least let me see you…"

"Nuh-uh! This time, you get to feel only, to touch and taste and hear." Her hands were at his jeans' fastening, one hand undoing it, the other rubbing him, between kisses and nibbles and words of more wonder and longing.

Only disjointed grunts, almost sobs, issued from him now. "Savannah—*querida*—just take me inside you…"

"Next time, darling, and the time after, and the time after that…" Her hands freed his engorged flesh. Pain and relief forced him under for a few seconds. He resurfaced to the feel of her lips. Surely she was damaging him for life! "I thought my memories had been lying to me, tormenting me. They were merciful, darling."

He almost had a seizure, yet he still resisted. He wanted to be inside her, the only place he belonged, the only pleasure he craved hers. Her tongue tasted him. "Let go, darling, give me this…"

Cruel. Merciless. The woman he worshipped. He roared the words to her, in Spanish, as swell after swell of agonized completion swept him.

A long time later, he lay under her worshipping hands and lips, still shuddering, still fully aroused. "Now you've had your way with me, will you untie me?"

"I haven't had my way with you yet."

"Then have it! Now, Savannah, *te lo ruego*, now…"

Her lips took the rest of his begging, his breath. He surged up, drove his tongue inside her mouth, showed her what he wanted to do to her body. Her cry went through him.

"*Querida*, if you won't let me loose then rub yourself against me, let me see what I do to you…"

"Oh, Javier, yes, darling. Tell me what you want to do to me."

"I want to devour you. I want to love you until you can't stand any more pleasure. And when you beg me to stop, I'll start again until you beg me never to stop."

"I never asked you to stop. Never will. More, Javier, tell me more…" She jumped up on top of the bed and stood between his legs. He watched every undulation of her silhouette striptease and told her more, everything he felt, everything he'd do to her. Her top was the last to go as she straddled his waist and rubbed her silk against his sides. She stretched up and shimmied out of it, swaying in a dance to the rocking rhythm of his heart. Then she leaned over and offered all of her skin to his, her breasts to his waiting mouth.

He'd never imagined anything like it. Even with her, from her. He filled his mouth with her beloved flesh, filled his soul with the music of her pleasure, spilling more passion for her gratification, until it was beyond endurance. "No more words, *querida*. You want more, I'll give it to you, give you everything, only if you take me."

"Javier—I've waited so long, wanted too much…" Her sob was stifled by his mouth.

"*Mi amor, te lo ruegole.* I beg you—let me see your face, just turn on the bedside lamp. I must see you."

She leaned across him and he caught at every part of her that touched him as she fulfilled his plea. Then it was there, the sight he'd missed as much as he would have the loss of all his limbs. Savannah. But she was better than all his memories now, in every way. And how she wanted him! Those heavenly eyes told him so. *Dying for you. Haven't been alive without you.*

His heart stampeded. He had to touch everything, taste every part.

"Untie me, Savannah!"

Too late. Time stopped as she began lowering herself on him, too slow, too tight, letting him see what taking him was doing to her.

Nothing mattered any more but watching her, giving her, giving in to her, to them. Like before, like never before. He fought against the brutal pleasure that forced his head back and his eyes closed. He needed to see it all. His memories had been false too. Her reality surpassed his dreams. Or was it love making everything different? Yes. Different, dominating—devastating.

She'd accommodated all of him and he thrust up into her, every lunge into her clinging flesh taking him deeper into dependence. How could he ever have less than her all now?

For now, he had her all. Her tears filling his mouth, her body convulsing around him in satisfaction, her voice breaking on his name, begging for the final giving, his seed inside her. By the time he was ready to give it, her second climax had her in its quaking grip. His roars of release intensified with her every spasm around him.

Frustration crashed on him the moment she fell on top of him.

"Release me, Savannah!"

Her mouth opened on his, her sensual giggle restoring his arousal to steel. "Didn't I already?"

"My hands, Savannah. *Now!*"

"You drive me wild when you growl." She tightened around him and he thrashed, throwing her off. If he didn't have his hands on her this second, he'd have a stroke.

Savannah tried to obey him and just slumped back on him, her hands feeling unmatched, unattached even. How did he expect her to function after what he'd done to her? And he'd done it tied up too. What would he have done had he had the use of his full body? *Untie him and find out.*

"Get scissors. In the nightstand." His snarl at her ineffective efforts sent her rummaging where he directed.

In seconds she'd freed his right hand and he snatched the scissors from her and did the rest. Her cries of "Oh, Javier, watch it! Slow down, *please*! You'll injure yourself!" accompanied his every wrench and slash.

At last he was free. And wild. Crouching on the bed, his shirt pooled at his wrists, openly predatory. His eyes threatened retribution, his every bunched muscle promising how well he'd carry it out, how hard, how long. Then he pounced. A shrill scream ripped from her, propelling her backwards, and she flew out of the room.

No pursuing footsteps came and she stilled for a second, heard a zip being done up. Then…thundering footsteps. He was still wearing his boots. She'd left them on, interested only in undressing him just enough to… Yes, enough *to*. Now to get away with it.

Too late. His breath was almost on her nape, his body moving the air at her back. Another yelp and a spurt of speed snatched her from his hands.

With his couch between them, they parried for a minute, then he bounded over it in a single leap. It still gave her the second she needed to scamper around it, run into another room.

It turned out to be the kitchen. More like kitchenette. Trapped!

He flicked on the single lamp over the kitchen table she was hiding behind, at leisure now. With only the tiny table between them, he stood there, his eyes brooding over her nakedness, planning all the ways he'd exploit it, his face a mask of taut, fierce arousal. A thrill of anticipation shook her.

His dark drawl was another blow to her molten core. "Bondage, S and M and now Catch. Any more games you want to play?"

"There was no S and M!"

"You don't consider leaving me there writhing, begging for my hands on you, to be sadistic? It was, believe me. I thought my head would blow off with frustration."

Was he angry?

His easy stroll towards her had her quaking. He reached for her and her teeth clattered together. He withdrew, a sharp move putting him at arm's length again. "What the…? Are you afraid, *querida*?"

Her answer was ready, incredulous. "Of you? Never! I was just worried…"

His face cleared again at her assurance, devilry igniting his eyes. "You should be worried."

He gathered her in his arms, nudged her thighs apart, half carried her to rest on his arousal. Apart from his open shirt showing off his massive torso and ridged abdomen, he was fully clothed, making her feel more than naked—exposed, vulnerable—and loving it. Knowing him, trusting him with her all, the game of domination and submission added another flavor to their sensual feast.

He let her slide down over him, then he pushed her back on the table, spread her legs, braced them at its edge and came between them, bending over her to plunge her into the deepest kiss he'd ever given her. Her soul flowed into him.

"Missed you, *mi corazón, mi amor*, starved for you. Now I get to feed again…" He escaped her clawing hands as she tried to undo his zipper, ignored her begging for him, slithered down her body, kissing and nibbling and suckling her all the way to her core. By the time his first finger slid inside her and his tongue started lashing her swollen flesh she was bucking, disintegrating with a permeating, numbing pleasure, her release complete—but it still wasn't enough. Only he would ever be enough, his closeness, his pleasure.

"Please, Javier, you, you, please…"

He caught the hands roaming his face, his shoulders, pinned them down. "No, you don't!"

Now she knew what he had felt, not being able to touch her. Her hands were burning. He dragged her limp body up with hands filled with controlled power and cherishing gentleness, turned her around and laid her facedown on the table.

She lay, hardly breathing, waiting for his payback. He took his time about it, reclaiming her every nerve and response and inch. He slid invisible touches down her back, tender licks and bites in lightning-inducing spots, whispered kisses all over her arms and nape and buttocks. As his touch heated, roughened, so did his words, his confessions of all the things that had gone through his mind since they'd met again. Her tears flowed out of her heart, at the beauty, the waste, the expectation.

When he had her in a state of continuous quivering, he withdrew. "You liked me helpless, didn't you?" He waited for her smothered wail of unbearable stimulation, her plea for him to just take her. "Why the rush? Aren't you enjoying your helplessness?"

"*No!*"

"Good!" His sonorous laugh peaked her distress, made her writhe back into him, desperate to take the lashing edge off the hunger.

Just when she thought something inside her would char, he rested his body on top of her back, whispered in her ear. "Do you want me now, *mi amor*?"

Her nod was frantic, her voice gone. He took pity on her then. He told her how he was going to take her, how he'd waited for this, how perfect she was as he spread her and started his gentle invasion, giving her time to gasp, to relax, to open and accommodate his size. Then he was assuaging her pangs, spreading deeper madness with every stroke, desperation with every deliberate withdrawal.

Her eyes caught glimpses of him when he bent to kiss and nip her nape and shoulders and cheeks, meeting his passion-driven gaze, the tension in her core spreading all through her, tightening, crushing her. She begged him again. He withdrew.

Before her scream of denial tore out of her, he turned her, slid her off the table and sprawled to the floor with her. Then he was there, thrusting inside her, hard now, no more games, giving her what she needed.

As she convulsed in his arms, their eyes locked. He let her watch him reaching his own explosive release inside her, filling her, filling all the places inside her body and soul that had been empty and would remain vacant for ever without him.

There would be no life without him now. Not really.

CHAPTER NINE

"WHAT do you really want from Javier?"

Savannah's head snapped up from her dinner at Tadeo's question. He'd kept his voice down, but everyone was much quieter today now there were only about forty people left. All of them knew exactly what she and Javier had been doing all last night and all day today.

Oh, why had they had to come back here?

Because a posse had been sent to fetch them for dinner, that was why!

Up until then, Javier had been rescuing her whenever anyone had launched an interrogation. She wasn't used to this. People normally butted into her life in subtle, political, far more destructive ways, not this tactless, harmless, distressing invasion of privacy. But this was one question she didn't want his help with. Didn't even want him to hear.

Three choices. Tell Tadeo to mind his own business, tell the truth, or stall. Stalling was all she could handle at the moment.

Arranging her features into a hopefully calm façade, she turned to Tadeo. "What I want is irrelevant. It's what he wants that matters now."

Tadeo's thick eyebrows shot up. "Are you for real? It's all about what women want. Men are just executors of your wills!"

She gave a wan smile at his play on words. "Not with this woman, or this man."

Tadeo was silent during dessert. Just as she thought he'd dropped the subject, he turned to her again, ultra-serious this time. "You refused him once. Why are you here after him again? When nothing has changed?"

Javier had told him of his proposal? Her gut twisted. "*I* have."

His eyes swept her, thoughtful, weighing. Then he nodded. "From what the guys who were with him in the US told me of you, I guess you have." Could this be more humiliating? "You still haven't answered my question."

She could just picture bashing him with the giant papaya and yelling for him to butt out. *Oh, just tell him. It's written all over you anyway.* "What do you think I want from him? What has Javier got to give me but himself? That's all I want. That's everything."

Tadeo's eyes stilled on her for a second, then his smile split his face from ear to ear. "Good. OK, you can hit me now!" His laugh rang out. "Oh, yes, you're transparent. But just think about it—when you and Javier are married, you'll have a lifetime of opportunities to bash me."

When you and Javier are married.

Tadeo's words ricocheted inside her for the rest of the evening, and all night as Javier deepened his claim on her soul, ravaged her senses and saturated her body with pleasure.

Near dawn, she was lying under him with *déjà vu* swamping her. It had been in exactly this position, in the aftermath of their last explosive joining, when he'd made his impetuous marriage proposal.

None would come from him now, or ever again, would it? He hadn't even said anything about feeling anything for her. And Tadeo thought their marriage was a certainty.

A breath at a time, remember?

Yeah, she remembered. She was counting on her memory to store up every breath with him, for the life she'd spend all alone…

*   *   *

"Can I have a word alone with you?"

What now? Savannah almost screamed in answer to Carmela's request. Another confessional? That would make how many in the last five days? Just what gave these people the right to interfere into their brother's life this way? Javier was thirty-eight, for heaven's sake. He could sleep with whomever he wanted without her passing their collective quality-testing first. No wonder Javier had chosen to buy a separate house nearby. No doubt to escape the committee deciding what he should eat for breakfast.

At least Carmela was asking to put her through the wringer in private.

Savannah's eyes darted to Javier. He was taking his leave from his parents and grandparents. Soon they'd be away from here. *So just get this over with.*

"Carmela, just tell me what you want, OK? You *are* going to tell me how wrong I am for Javier and to leave him alone, aren't you?"

Carmela's eyes widened with embarrassment.

Savannah sighed. So she was right. The men seemed to have come to accept her since her conversation with Tadeo. It had been a relief that they'd stopped watching and probing her. It had also been an extra twist of the knife, this seeming consensus she'd be one of them soon. But the women, on the other hand…

Carmela cleared her throat, started. "I like you, Savannah. I think you're a good, courageous woman, trying to do a very hard thing. For every one of my people you've helped, I thank you."

Sounded good so far. But the next words were bound to tell her why she was still all wrong.

Sure enough, those words followed, Carmela's features apologetic as she said them. "But this is still an adventure to you. To Javier it's his life. He should be rich—he would be if the tons of money he makes didn't all go to humanitarian ends. You'll say money isn't an issue since you have plenty of it, but if you marry him, he'll insist on being the provider. Can you live here, in his house, on what he considers is enough for both of you?''

Savannah opened her mouth to tell her marriage wasn't even an option, but Carmela mistook her aggravated look for defense and pressed on her attack. "You may think you can put up with it but, believe me, life is hard here. Oh, there are areas in Colombia where you'd never believe anything wrong is going on in the country, where there is beauty and prosperity, but this is never where Javier will be. I'm used to having the simplest in life, and I wouldn't last living the way he does. The best you can have with him is a short-lived marriage before you buckle under the hardships. I want you to consider the day you'd come to resent Javier and end up leaving him, maybe after there are children, too.''

Children. Javier's.

Oh, God, please get me out of here.

But Carmela wasn't finished. "I know you want Javier now. Women—they all go crazy for him.'' Just what Savannah needed now: to know how run-of-the-mill, one-of-a-herd she was. Not that that was news. But what followed was. "But you've come at a time when Javier has started to…notice the woman who wants to be his helpmeet in the difficult path he's chosen. She's one who expects nothing from life but to love him, who'll bear him as many children as he wants, a woman who calls Colombia home and can never leave it.''

Another woman? And he had started to…*notice* her? As in, already intimate with her?

Vicious fangs clamped in her guts. Jealousy. The one thing she hadn't suffered on Javier's account. He'd never given her cause. There'd been no doubt he was a one-woman man. As long as he remained with that woman.

But had he been forming a relationship when she'd barged into his life, forced her presence on him? Had that been why he'd been so reluctant to act on his desires? His purely sexual desires? Until she'd imposed herself on him, while he'd literally been tied up?

Don't let me start weeping now, oh, God—please!

Javier was striding towards them now, his intimate smile wrenching at the tatters inside her. Without one more glance towards Carmela she ran towards him, heard the manic note in her quivering voice. ''Are we ready to go at last?''

Are we ready to go at last?

Javier put his full strength into hurling the rock. He heard the crack of his shoulder at the violent, inappropriate, *stupid* action, then the rock's as it hit the surface of the river.

Savannah's feverish words hadn't stopped revolving in his brain over the last five days now, eating at him with each cycle.

What a fool he'd been.

He'd thought there had been a chance, after that first day—and night—back in Neiva that she wasn't too repelled by his family or his house, that she'd get along to a degree and might actually consider including them in her life. He'd drowned in her passion and had waited for some sign, some word, that it was more than passion this time, that if he asked now, she wouldn't laugh again.

But she wouldn't laugh this time. She would gasp in horror.

She'd been almost *crazy* to leave. She would never return, not voluntarily, and must be very sorry she'd asked him to take her there. Her eyes had been rabid as she'd tossed a wave at his family before jumping in the Jeep as if she'd been escaping something revolting, suffocating…

''Javier, we need to expand the MSU now. There's a glitch in the mechanism.''

At Alonso's call, Javier turned from the sorry sight that was adding to his depression—the twisted, destroyed bridge on the Magdalena River. Another scar of the ongoing war between government troops and drug-financed rebel groups in San Vicente del Caguán.

Maldita sea! Even without being exposed to his own life, Savannah had already seen and experienced enough to convince her to run home the moment her mission was over. He'd be crazy to ask her to stay. Even if she loved him, this was no place for her. And anyway, she didn't love him.

Javier slowed down as he fell into step with Alonso, to make allowance for his awkward gait. He'd long begged Alonso's forgiveness in public for threatening him with physical violence, no matter what the reason. In private, he'd also told him about Caridad's emotions for him. Alonso had heard him out then had walked out without a word. He'd behaved as if nothing had happened ever since.

To break the uneasy silence on the way back, Javier found nothing but a rhetorical question. "So we're ready to start our first list?"

Alonso gave him the deserved ridicule. "No, we're expanding the MSU to play squash."

"*Touché.* So—when are you going to forgive me?"

"You mean for making me feel inferior and crippled?"

"*Por Dios*, Alonso. It never, ever crossed my mind that you are. And you aren't. I would have threatened Esteban with the same thing, and we both know who'd win there. That was about defending Caridad, not putting you down."

Alonso gave a mirthless laugh. "You managed to do it nevertheless."

Javier was mortified. What was there to offer now but more protestations of good intentions, when they'd already led to hell?

"But I do forgive you for that, Javier. I do know it's my own insecurities putting the worst possible interpretation on your words. Hell, not pussyfooting around my fragile ego means you *don't* consider me any less macho or sturdy than you are."

OK. Good. *Great.* But? There was a but here.

"What I don't forgive you for is planting this crazy, damaging hope that Caridad could love me."

Javier came to an abrupt stop, took Alonso by the shoulders. "That's not a crazy hope. The woman is lovesick for you."

Alonso shook his head. "Stop it, Javier. If you want to pander to my ego, you're doing the one thing that's bound to damage it further."

"*You* stop it, Alonso. You may be so insecure you can't see it, but we can *all* see how much she loves you and craves one gentle word from you. She as much as told me that, after she gave me a piece of her mind—can you believe that? Caridad railing at me for being so hard on you?"

Sudden tears filled Alonso's eyes. Two overflowed. His choking whisper closed Javier's already oppressed chest. "Really?"

"Yes, really."

"But—but why would she love me? I have nothing."

"You have everything, Alonso. You're a brilliant doctor and an honorable, handsome, strong man…"

"Don't go overboard now, Javier. Handsome? Strong?" Alonso's gaze went to his shortened leg.

"Give me a break, Alonso. Are you comparing yourself to me? To anyone with matching legs? What about those without any? And if I lost one or both my legs tomorrow, would that make me less of a man?"

"No. But as a lover, in a woman's eyes, in a beautiful, perfect woman's eyes…"

Would Savannah look at *him* if he weren't big and strong and capable in bed? Probably not. *Most certainly not.* But Caridad wasn't Savannah.

"Why don't you ask Caridad? She'll tell you what she sees in you."

Alonso was silent for a second. "If she loves me then she's

a fool. She could have her pick of powerful and wealthy men. Someone who'd help her whole family, not barely support her."

"That's her choice, isn't it? And, then, you're not making money because you're following me around in my non-profit escapades. Work in a private hospital and you'll be able to support Caridad's horde. That's a humanitarian cause, and you'd be helping the woman you love while you're at it."

"You make it all sound so easy."

"It is, you lucky man!"

But luck had nothing to do with it. It was all about choices. Alonso had chosen the local Cinderella to fall in love with. *He* had to go fall in love with an enchantress from another world.

Alonso fell silent, pondering the new possibilities. A few meters from the MSU, he spoke again. "Am I allowed to talk about you and Savannah now?"

No, Javier wanted to shout it. But right now he would have let Alonso walk over him, just to get him out of his funk, to make amends. His "go ahead" smile was more of a grimace.

"Nothing went according to your pessimistic projections, huh? Savvy is amazing, and seeing you together is even more so. It got me so lonely for Caridad I wanted to jump in the river."

"Now you get to jump in Caridad's arms instead."

"Not as soon as you get to jump in Savvy's!" He tossed his head in the MSU's direction. Savannah was standing in the vestibule, waiting for them, lithe, golden, radiating passion and promise.

He didn't climb up the ladder. Her magnetism pulled him up, and into her waiting arms. Her hands went to his head, performing that curious ritual of hers, kissing his forehead first. Love swelled inside him, flowed to arms that swept her up, to lips that gasped for hers. The taste of her eagerness flooded him and he sank, wishing he'd never resurface.

But he had to. There were the claps and the whistles on one hand, the job on the other. He clung to her lower lip for one farewell suckle then let her go.

He went to tackle the expansion mechanism problem with Emmanuel and she joined him, her hand in his. In minutes they were stepping out of the MSU as it expanded.

"Did you draw up a list for today?" Javier asked.

"While you were throwing rocks in the river, you mean?" She pinched his buttock. "Sure did, beautiful."

He choked. Would she ever stop surprising him?

Sí, in nineteen days.

"Beautiful? *Me?*"

'Yes, you. The most beautiful thing on earth. The amazing thing is you don't have a clue you are. It's one of the things I love about you."

Love?

He didn't know what kept him on his feet. Then he was swept off them as everyone joined them and carried him along and back into the MSU. Everything, even his agitation and disbelief, had to be put on hold then, as they prepared their stations for their first surgery list, and as they were submerged in it.

He was separated from Savannah all through the list. By the time she joined him for the last procedure of their evening list, a laparoscopic cholecystectomy, he was at roaring pitch. She'd said she loved watching him in his field of expertise, minimally invasive surgery, loved learning at his hands. All he wanted to know, all he'd been able to think about for the last eight hours, was: did she love *him*? Had she really meant it, or had it been just a figure of speech? Would this day ever end so he could find out?

Her throaty voice broke over him. "A straightforward case for a change?"

His eyes clung to hers, searching. "*Sí.* Chronic cholecystitis, with intermittent upper-quadrant abdominal pain, nausea, weight loss and tenderness on palpation. Ultrasound showed the gallbladder stones, three of them, big ones, around two centimeters each. Gallbladder wall thickness around three and a half millimeters.''

''Where do you want me?'' She meant at which port of the four he was going to access the patient's abdomen from. He knew where *he* wanted her. Her eyes fervently agreed and her lips mouthed, 'Soon!'

Javier struggled to clear his throat, and his head. Alonso had already completed the general anesthesia. ''I'm obtaining a standard four-port access. One 1 cm umbilical port, one 1 cm epigastric, and two 0.5 cm right upper quadrant. You can take those. I'll start with the umbilical...'' He paused as he performed the small incision, produced the carbon dioxide tube nozzle and inflated the abdomen with it, for better viewing when he introduced the long flexible tube with the laparoscopic video camera on its end, and to provide more room to maneuver during the surgery. ''OK. Camera in. You're on.''

Savannah made the tiny incisions and introduced the two fenestrated blunt forceps that they'd use to maneuver their way to the gallbladder. Her eyes swung up to him after he'd finished making the epigastric incision. ''So what's the story with San Vicente del Caguán?''

Javier started dissecting the inflamed, adherent gallbladder out of its fat pad and from the liver's surface, watching his actions, which the camera transmitted to the monitor. ''Savannah, the gallbladder is too distended. Insert a needle and drain some bile so I can apply a clamp grasper for dissection and manipulation.''

She did that in under a minute and he started talking as he dissected the short cystic duct free, the duct connecting the gallbladder to the common bile duct, using a right-angle clamp. ''When the peace process with Colombia's largest armed opposition group ended, the government ordered the aerial bombardment of the guerrillas' safe haven, what used to be called the demilitarized zone. Then they started reclaiming it.''

Javier maneuvered clips on the cystic duct away from the common bile duct, then Savannah transected it using scissors. ''San Vicente del Caguán was one of five municipalities that made up the DMZ. It served as the guerrilla army's capital. When visitors started pouring in following the suspension of hostilities, the town's economy boomed. Then the security forces retook the urban centers, resulting in massive civilian casualties, and everything fell apart.''

He paused as they repeated the same technique with the cystic artery, dissecting it free using a right-angle clamp and dividing it between clips.

''The government promised San Vicente del Caguán would be protected from retaliation. Instead, it was abandoned, by both the Colombian authorities and the international community. The civilian population was also stigmatized as 'pro-guerrilla'. Everyone conveniently forgot about the guerrillas' persistent human-rights violations when they were in control of the DMZ.''

He performed the hook electrocautery to dissect the gall-bladder off the liver bed and Savannah irrigated for him with normal saline, suctioned off the fluid and clots, checked the dissected area for hemostasis, making sure there was no bleeding. ''OK, Savannah, insert a soft four-millimeter silastic drain through the lateral port, to ensure all of the washout fluid is removed early in the post-operative period.''

He handed the gallbladder from forceps to clawed grabber, then drew it out of the abdomen through the umbilical port, very careful to avoid rupturing it while pulling. ''Violence escalated when the military retook the area, and the civilian population have been systematically targeted, both by the security forces and their paramilitary allies, and by the guerrillas. Harassment, torture, threats, kidnappings for ransom, killings—political and non-political—are all on the rise, though it's difficult to gauge the extent, due to the wall of fear and silence. Unknowns in the area are also targeted, in the general atmosphere of paranoia and opportunism.''

He met Savannah's eyes, saw her acknowledgment of his meaning, the possible hazards of being here. She dropped her gaze first as she removed the epigastric port. He exhaled, closed the umbilical port, removed the other ports and ensured hemostasis, wrapping up the procedure.

"Twenty minutes! That has to be some record, Dr. Sandoval.'' Nikki sounded too cheerful. Probably scared out of her wits.

"You sure are the fastest surgeon I've seen.'' Savannah's praise was as potent as everything about her, always making him want to jump up and punch the air. As she walked behind him to the soiled room, her whisper hit him between his shoulder blades. "Not fast at all in other capacities—to my eternal gratitude.''

He turned on her, pushed her back into the soiled room, snatched her cap and surgical gown off, then his, and took her lips. His tongue prodded them open, then drove into her.

He came up at Nikki's discreet cough, heard Savannah gasping, giggling. She gave his jaw one last nibble before she slipped out of his arms. As they washed, her sideways glance tantalized him further. "I take it you don't want to have dinner?''

He herded her out, dragged her behind him, running all the way to her tent. "If I say I want *you* for dinner, it won't be true. I want you for, before and after every meal, every day, *mi amor*. I want you every moment of every day.''

There. He'd as good as said he wanted her always, for always.

What would she say?

She said nothing. Just fell on her sleeping bag, every frantic move she made as she worked off her boots and pants ar-

ranging her in a pose that blanked his mind with carnal fe-
rocities. He'd take her like that first, before she managed to
take off her shirt, suckle her through it and the bra. It sent
her crazy when he did that. Then he'd have her on top…

Just ask her before all your mental operations fail.

He fell to his knees before her and she surged into him,
ripping his shirt open, her mouth latching on to his quivering
muscles, biting, suckling hard. He didn't ask. He roared.

"Don't be mad." Her smile went through him, a spotlight
of pure delight illuminating his soul. His hand convulsed in
her hair, pressing her head harder into him as she suckled his
nipple. If only he could just drive her into his chest, where
he could keep her for ever. "I'll hunt for the buttons and sew
them back on—as usual."

"I never thought…you'd be…such a seamstress." His
gasps rose as she pushed him down and straddled him.

"No? But you always praise my suturing skills. It's all
needlework."

Her moist heat ignited him and the overriding drive to
merge with her *now* took over. A laugh erupted from deep in
his chest at her gasps as he switched their positions. He tore
her shirt open, revealing her heaving breasts. "*I'll* sew these
buttons back on." He tugged again, shredding it. "I'll perform a damn esthetic repair."

Her cotton bra and panties met the same fate. He freed
himself, put a hand under each of her knees and dragged her
over him. He opened her thighs around his waist as he knelt
between them, her hips on his thighs. He rested himself at her
entrance, soaked up her quivering anticipation, the crashing
waves of her desire through the contact. His eyes squeezed
shut as a groan reverberated through both their bodies. Then
he sought her eyes. A tear slipped from her right one into her
trembling mouth, emerged on a delicate, overpowering
"*Please!*"

He rammed into her. Her scream at his abrupt invasion

drenched him in dread. What if it was pain and not pleasure? He tried to pull out but her clamping legs kept him close, her pulsing body kept him inside her. "No, darling, no—please— just give me…"

"Mi amor, mi vida!" He obeyed her. The tension was already crackling, lightning bolts of impending release flashing in his system. Her cries, telling him how he felt inside her, what he made her feel, filled his head, each cry another sledgehammer of stimulation.

"Javier, *Javier*…" Her cries choked as he picked up pace and ferocity. He absorbed her every shudder and twist and grimace as all her tension tightened her beloved body into an upward bow. Then he thrust her over the edge, and bore the storm of her release until her convulsions broke his own dam. She pushed herself up on extended arms and he lunged into her kiss, poured all his love, all of himself into her.

She slumped back and they remained like that, coming down together, merged in ultimate intimacy, her thighs stroking his sides, her sated smile stroking his soul, his hands and eyes roving over her in a soothing, reverent ritual.

They hadn't used protection. Not once. The need to ask was constantly there. Was she using birth control? If she had been from the start—*why*? If she wasn't, then—then…

An image of a baby girl with moonbeam hair and heaven-colored eyes burgeoned inside him, pushing aside everything, taking precedence.

Ask her. Offer her. Everything that you are.

And what was that? Strife and danger and exhaustion? In exchange for what? This? What was this to her? Sex? How long would it last?

But she said she loves you.

Figure of speech. Savannah would tell you straight if she did. And even if she does, how long will that last?

He bent, collected her to his body, sat with her wrapped around him, buried his face in her neck. She flowed around him, blanketing him with serenity and simmering passion, imbuing him with resolve.

He *would* make it last. He would keep her with him. There was a way. There had to be. He just hadn't found it yet.

But he would.

Savannah accommodated Javier deeper into the curve of her neck, into her depths, tightened her hold around him inside and out. She stroked his silky hair, his velvet muscled back and arms and thighs, wondered again at how smooth and polished he was, his native American legacy. She wondered what was going on in his powerful mind.

She'd as good as told him she loved him today, this time in words. She'd told him in every other way in the past ten days. He hadn't reciprocated.

Oh, he had, incessantly, every time they made love. *Mi amor, mi vida, mi corazón, mi alma.* His love and life and heart and soul. And, boy, did he sound convincing. But that was only during delirium. When they were out of bed, everything he did said he couldn't wait for the next time, that it was always on his mind, that he loved being with her, working with her, counting on her. Did that amount to love?

Not really. A lot remained. Believing in her enough to ask her again, for one. Trusting her with his name and honor and children, for another. Wanting her for more than now, wanting her for ever…

"*Mi amor*, you're uncomfortable." Javier must have felt her tensing. He laid her back, massaged her cramped thighs, his tender touch relaxing her then winding her up again. Then he loved her again, long, long and gentle, building to the same ferocity, the same sweeping, annihilating release. Then he surrounded her, slept.

Sleep didn't descend on her. The ticking in her head that was counting down her remaining time in Colombia always kept her awake. Carmela's revelations had accelerated the ticking and made her frantic, if only for a couple of days after they'd left Neiva. Disregarding Carmela's warnings had been easy when Javier acted as if no other woman existed, not only in his life but in the world.

But that's what men do when they're cheating. Remember Mark? All over you at night, all over his nurse in the morning?

No—Javier wasn't like that. His integrity ran all through him. If there was another woman, he hadn't made any promises to her, hadn't even raised her expectations. He hadn't been intimate with her, not even familiar. She knew it, believed it. He wasn't capable of pettiness or duplicity, of such disrespect to a woman. She wasn't hurting another woman, being with him.

But she also believed there *was* such another woman, a hopeful, a candidate for the position of his wife, picked and approved by his family. Convenient, conservative, conventional.

Well, tough! There was no prior claim, and she was damned if she was giving him up to any convenient "helpmeet". To anyone!

She was the woman who sent him into frenzies of desire, who satisfied him out of his mind, the one who challenged him, made him dissolve in laughter, provoked and sustained his interest, his respect. She was, and always wanted to be, his partner.

What had that other woman done to deserve him? She was convenient by an accident of birth. Her life expectations were so limited that Javier was a dream come true to her, and any hardship in living with him would be a luxury.

But Savannah had chosen to be who she was now. Her choices had been open, and she'd chosen his path. Hardships with him would be neither adversity nor luxury, but quests, challenges, aspirations. She'd gone on a quest and she'd discovered her strength, had found herself. Now she was as self-made as he was. That made her his equal at last. That was what a true partner was. That was what Javier deserved, what he must want. He wouldn't stomach an inferior, a dependant, but would only consider being with a match. And that was her.

What was more, that other woman could make do with any other man. She couldn't. For her, it was Javier or nothing.

She had to believe that, if he had a place in him and in his life for a woman at all, it would be her he'd choose. Even if he hadn't made a new offer.

Suddenly it hit her. He might be afraid to make one. Considering her reaction the last time, she couldn't blame him.

Fairness dictated she even out the balance. It was her turn to ask.

''What was it you said again?'' Savannah adjusted the scarf over her hair, unsettled by the way the guerrilla's eyes were glued to the tendrils that had escaped. ''You spoke too quickly.''

''Are you American?''

She flashed her MSU credentials at him. ''I am a doctor— a surgeon. I am with the MSU visiting San Vicente del Caguán. Those are my patients. As you can see, one of them is critically ill.''

The guerrilla was withdrawing, about to let them go on their way, when his colleague, a younger guerrilla who didn't look a day over seventeen, talked to him, this time in Spanish so fast it went over her head.

The older guerrilla shoved his face into hers again. ''You will come with us.''

OK, don't show any sign of unease or revulsion. ''I and my team will be at your disposal in any medical services, as soon as we take care of our patients.''

"We only want you. But I guess the rest will have to come along, too."

Damn. So *this* was what she'd felt half an hour ago. The foreboding that heralded a catastrophe. She'd mistaken her emergency for it.

She should have waited for Javier, for any of the others. Now this checkpoint had materialized on their usual route, just when she'd decided to transfer her patient back to the MSU with only Caridad along.

But she'd had to do it. When the emergency had arrived, Javier had been busy in the local clinic, continuing the hands-on training of the only doctor there, in the middle of a surgical procedure using the facility's capabilities. He had Alonso with him, while Luis and Miguel had been similarly involved. Esteban was with the rest of the guards back in the MSU. Come to think of it, it might have been even worse if any of them had been along. Things might have gotten violent and out of control. This way Javier was safe and free. He'd get them out of this.

"Follow us."

In a minute she had guerrilla vehicles in front and behind her, and the young guerrilla beside her, squeezing Caridad in the back with their patient, his wife and two sons.

Alert Javier before they take you out of cell phone range, before they take away the cell phone itself.

The phone was in the left pocket of her baggy pants. She felt for its pads through the fabric. The green handset pad for dialing—here, and Javier's number had been the last she'd dialed. She hit it.

She started talking to the guerrilla so he wouldn't hear Javier's voice when he answered the phone. "So, what did you say to your partner that made him change his mind about letting us go?"

The young guerrilla shifted in his seat, looked out of the

Jeep. Had her question made him uncomfortable? "I just told him who you are. I recognized you from TV."

TV? GAO and local authorities weren't airing footage of the MSU mission complete with photos!

The guerrilla's next words made it all clear. "I watch international channels. It was a commercial, from a very big American health group. They said you were one of them, and you were in Colombia with the MSU."

Oh, no, no! Her father was using her presence here as propaganda for Richardson Health Group!

She hoped he'd be satisfied when his propaganda coup cost him his daughter.

She looked at the young man. Would he be her killer?

No time for morbid projections now. Get Javier as much information as you can.

She raised her chin at the guerrilla, along with her voice. "So you know me. Mind telling me who you are, now you've kidnapped us?"

CHAPTER TEN

KIDNAPPED.

Javier stared ahead, kept his cell phone glued to his ear. Savannah's voice was filtering through engine and road noises, filling his head. Something hot and wet and blinding burst in there, with every word he heard.

It wasn't true. None of it. He had to be hallucinating. It had to be him fearing for Savannah too much, living in dread of all sorts of worst-case scenarios. She was next door—next door…

The local doctor's exclamation echoed from another reality. Javier looked down at him, at the patient with the half-drained abscess, at Alonso's alarmed face, and realized he'd leapt to his feet and knocked over the surgical tray.

"Just keep on, just—just…" No more words came, just blind panic, propelling him, seeking Savannah. *Savannah.*

She wasn't next door. She'd taken an impending perforating appendicitis patient, and Caridad, and had gone back to the MSU. And she'd been kidnapped.

Kidnapped.

His Savannah, surrounded by rabid beasts, like that first night. This time he wasn't there to hack the monsters who'd abducted her to pieces and—and… *Dios*, what would they do to her? What were they doing to her now…?

His mind blinked on and off, attempting to ward off panic and desperation and their insidious whispers to fall to his knees and let madness consume him.

No. No despair, no taking refuge in breakdown. His precious, brilliant Savannah had called out to him, had warned him and given him vital information. She needed his strength, his stability. She'd sense it, as she always sensed danger and disaster. And, as those always made her cold and anxious, his determination would warm her, steady her, sustain her until she was back in his arms. And she would be. She *would*.

Mi vida, *I'm saving you, no matter what!*

"What did you say?" Savannah focused on Caridad's pale face. Caridad repeated her question and Savannah still only heard Javier's voice, soothing, bolstering. She must be wishing for it so hard she was imagining it. Or was she breaking down?

No—she wasn't that agitated. Oh, she was afraid, fully realized the mortal danger they were in. But she felt nothing like that night in the woods. She wasn't panicking like Caridad, or resigned to her fate like her patient and his family...

Her patient! He was all that mattered now. The man had to have an immediate appendectomy or die.

She gave Caridad's hand a reassuring squeeze and surged up to her feet. "You. Diaz!"

Their young guard snapped around, his slanting black eyes widening at her tone, at her moving against his superior's orders.

"Tell General Gomes I need to operate on Señor Herrera right now!"

General Gomes was just coming in, and heard her imperious order. "Well, Dr. Richardson, you may be a high-and-mighty American doctor, but here you're just our hostage." His semi-automatic weapon jabbed her hard in her right shoulder, sending her stumbling backwards. "Sit down and shut up."

Images of scratching the man's eyes out flashed in her mind. *Not wise. At least, not now.* She recovered from her stumble, came back in his face. "You may want only me as a hostage, but the more the merrier, right? People will negotiate for *him*, too. Any money's better than nothing."

The big, coarse mercenary bristled. "You don't need to be

in one piece when we return you to your people, you know? *If* we return you.''

OK. She knew the odds. She shrugged. ''What have you got to lose? Just let me save him now, then you can kill us all later anyway.''

''Are you out of your mind, *mujer*? You think you can perform surgery here?''

''That's for me to worry about. Do I have your permission to go ahead?''

Gomes looked over at his men, laughed. ''Oh, why not? This should be a lot of laughs, watching you cut that bastard open.''

The men all laughed on cue. Savannah's heart bounded with urgency. ''The show won't start without the supplies bag in our Jeep.''

''Get her what she wants, *hombres*. And get me a chair. I'm sitting through this one!''

In ten minutes, their audience was assembled, Herrera's family were sobbing in the corner and Savannah and Caridad had him on the floor and were kneeling on either side of him, preparing for the procedure.

''Dr. Richardson, are you sure about this?''

Caridad's wavering whisper trembled down Savannah's spine. Of course she wasn't sure. Under any other conditions, an appendectomy was a piece of cake. But she didn't have the necessary equipment or drugs, the septic conditions were horrifying and Herrera's condition was deteriorating. And she'd never handled anesthesia herself.

There's no other choice. Do it, and do it quickly!

She had already intubated Herrera using thiopental, the quickest-acting IV anesthetic. But it was very short-acting. To attain and maintain anesthesia deep enough for abdominal surgery, she needed an inhalational anesthetic. Which she didn't have.

Up his analgesia, add a powerful muscle relaxant.

"Caridad, another ten milligrams each of morphine and suc-
cinylcholine."

Caridad's eyes widened. "That will paralyze his respiratory
muscles!"

Which meant he wouldn't be able to breathe on his own
and would need manual ventilation with the bag-mask. She
couldn't have Caridad doing that while assisting her. She
needed another pair of hands. "Diaz, come here!"

The boy looked at his superior. Gomes nodded and Diaz
ran to her.

"Count one, two, three and on four give him a breath—
like this." The boy nodded nervously. She turned to the
crowd. "I need your sharpest blade." She had suture material,
forceps, scissors, but no scalpels.

A dozen daggers and switchblades were held out to her.
She liked the vicious-looking saber strapped to Gomes's leg.
"General, if I may?"

He handed it to her with a "you're crazy" smile.

Probably. "Now a lighter."

Again, a dozen lighters were offered. She snatched the first
one, heated the blade until it glowed red.

She took in a deep breath. It got trapped in her lungs.
Steady! "Caridad…" *Steady!* "I go in, you suction. After
bleeding abates, you swab and hand me instruments. If the
appendix has ruptured you irrigate copiously, so ready three
saline bags." She turned to their audience. She lacked another
thing. A retractor. "I need another volunteer."

Gomes himself rose this time. All right. Let him do something useful for once in his life. She handed him povidine.
"Wash your hands with that, then put those gloves on. Once
I make my incision, I need you to keep the wound edges apart
so I can get to the appendix."

She performed a three-inch incision. Her hand trembled.
Not agitated? Ha.

But as she deepened her access through the layers of the
abdominal wall, she lost herself to her task as usual, every-

thing else ceasing to register, to matter. Her nerves steadied as she snapped orders to her assistants, modifying their positions and actions, locating the appendix and searching for additional problems. Finding none, she freed the appendix from its attachment to the colon, ligating and cutting it then stapling the colon hole. The appendix hadn't ruptured, though it would have in just a few more minutes. But an abscess had formed. She placed drains to siphon off the pus then raced through abdominal closure as Herrera began to move.

Caridad topped off analgesia in his IV drip then raised her eyes to Savannah. What next?

What next for them? Savannah only had answers concerning the surgery. "Usual post-operative drill, just double the antibiotic cover and tetanus toxoid and keep the ITT in for now. Well done!" Savannah turned to Diaz and Gomes. "You gentlemen handled yourselves like pros. Well done to you, too!"

Gomes was all incredulity. "You mean he isn't going to die?"

Savannah gave him a long look. "No. Are we?"

"Are we agreed?"

Javier looked into the guerrilla leader's cold eyes, squashing down all his frustration and rage, all his personal terror and murderous animosity. Telling the man what he thought of him, just before beating him to death, would sabotage Savannah's chances of getting out of this unharmed. Out of this at all.

Take the offer, you bastard. Make the exchange.

"We're no such thing, Dr. Sandoval."

Javier gritted his teeth. "You want money—here it is. But it's *my* ransom, not Dr. Richardson's. Let her go now and take me, and you'll get even more money on my release. I would advise you not to hold out for money from her people. Whatever money you get for her from them would only open the gates of hell on you. The Richardsons don't only have money, they have political power. No one gets away with threatening one of their own, or with taking their money. And if you've harmed her…''

I'll rip your neck out right now and be done with it!

''She's unharmed. Gomes, my second in command, the one who caught her, tells me he thinks no one would harm her even if he ordered them to. She's made quite an impression, that one.''

Savannah. Savannah, mi amor. The blow of longing and fear almost drove Javier to his knees. But he couldn't afford to let the man witness his weakness, give him more advantages. He persisted. ''They'll have no such qualms with me, which will only strengthen your position. So will you take me instead? Let her and the others go?''

''I don't want you, or your friend here.'' His bored gaze swept from Javier to the fidgeting Alonso. ''The last thing I need is more hostages. I need cash.''

''So what's wrong with the cash I brought along?''

''Two hundred and fifty thousand dollars for her release and another on yours isn't bad, but I was hoping for more. You have to understand we're financing the fight for freedom, for social reform. We have great expenses. Still…''

Would his skull burst with rage and outrage? *Keep it to yourself, don't antagonize him. He's wavering.*

Javier started to stress the advantages of taking his offer now, and General Mendoza's cell phone rang.

The man sauntered out of earshot, returned after ten minutes of involved conversation, all smiles. ''God is on our cause's side. I just got a better offer from her people. After five days of failure to reach them, I'd almost given up hope.''

Javier closed his eyes. Would that help? Or would it only complicate matters now? Would the Richardsons just hand over the money, or would they play some trick that would leave Savannah open to retaliation? Every gruesome possibility swamped his mind. He forced his jaw open to deliver the question. ''What's their offer?''

"Five million dollars. Tomorrow."

"Who made the offer?"

"Her husband."

Javier almost doubled over with shock.

Her husband.

Mark.

He still called himself that. Did he know what he was talking about? Was she going back to him?

Just get her out now. Worry about who she'll return to when she's safe.

"And you are going to take their offer? You will let her go tomorrow?"

Mendoza looked at him for a long moment. "I'll get back to you. Now, I'll take your contribution to our cause, Doctor, if you don't mind."

Javier released his hold on the briefcase, turned and got back into the Jeep, his every muscle quivering with hope and fury and dread. Esteban waited only for Alonso to get in before he roared away from the rendezvous Mendoza had picked to discuss Javier's offer in person.

The last person Javier expected or wanted to see was waiting for them at the MSU.

Mark.

Alonso and Esteban had been silent all the way back. The way they disappeared, leaving him alone with Mark, said they'd already guessed he was that husband General Mendoza had talked about.

Javier stepped down from the Jeep slowly, trying to harness his aggression and despair.

"Dr. Sandoval, I'm Dr. Mark Atkinson, Savannah's—"

"*Ex*-husband." Javier ignored the extended hand. He was damned if he'd shake the man's hand. He wasn't that civilized. "I know. I hope you don't have the ransom with you."

Mark raised his eyebrows, answering aggression in his

eyes. "I hope I'm not so stupid as to walk around the Colombian wilderness with five million dollars in cash. How did your meeting with Mendoza go?"

"It was going well, until you stepped in and flashed the big bucks at him."

The man straightened, almost matching Javier's six feet three, returning his assessing glance. Class and wealth oozed out of his every super-groomed pore. But Mark Atkinson was no soft yuppie. Tough, good-looking, his cool grey eyes radiated intelligence and determination. He had everything. Damn him.

That man had known Savannah in total intimacy. He wanted her still. Would he get her? Could Javier bring his jealousy under control long enough to talk to the man without tackling him to the ground and pummeling his handsome face to a pulp?

"You think he was going to let her go for a quarter of a million dollars?"

"He was about to buckle and settle for my money. Now, with five million dollars involved, anything can happen."

"He'll take it. And tomorrow Savannah will be free."

"Now you've offered that much money, he's liable to hang on to her, to milk more money from you. With me, he knew I offered all I could ever get—with you, the sky's the limit."

"He'll only get the money once we're certain she's in the clear. Savannah's father is back in Bogotá, orchestrating everything, and I've got Washington's top hostage negotiator with me…"

"No! You and your mercenaries keep out of this. *I'll* negotiate, *I'll* set up the meeting place, deliver the ransom and bring her back. I'm not letting you try anything that may jeopardize her in any way."

"I wouldn't jeopardize Savannah. I love her…"

"Not as much as I do! Not a fraction as much as I do! I would *die* for her. Or worse. I went today to do just that. I'll do it again and again. Would you?"

No. He wouldn't. He'd never dream of endangering himself in the least for her, his image-completing partner. Mark's eyes made the confession, flashed hostility at Javier for forcing the admission from him. Then he drew in a deep inhalation, relaxed with a visible effort. "The money will be available to you as soon as you set up a release time with Mendoza."

Javier nodded, turned away, unable to look at Mark any more. Mark's agitated words hit him in the back in one vicious blow. "When you get her out, you won't *really* get her. She isn't here for you. She's here to teach me and her father a lesson. She'll go to any lengths to get back at us, to spite us, to break all our rules and expectations. Nothing is extreme enough to achieve her point—leaving her job, her country, sleeping with you—even getting herself killed."

It would kill him. One more hour like the last beyond desperate six days, not knowing, imagining the worst, prey to every incapacitating, mind-destroying emotion he had no name for.

Die later. Get her out first. And he would, as soon as that damned bastard Mendoza phoned.

Javier jumped, imagining his cell phone was ringing again—but this time it was ringing for real!

He had no breath, no voice to answer with. Dios, *please*!

General Mendoza's voice crackled over the bad connection. "Dr. Sandoval, I've decided to take your offer."

The world seemed to stop. He couldn't be hearing what he wanted to hear, could he?

"My research says you're right. Whatever I get from the Richardsons now, they'll spend far more just to get even. And also I can't wait to get your Dr. Richardson off my hands. So I'll consider your offering to be a fellow patriot's generous donation to our cause, and that will be the end of it. Your people will be returned at sunset, where we met before."

Elation, trepidation and disbelief muted Javier. General

Mendoza went on. "No surprises, Sandoval. Just take your woman and forget about us."

"What about us? We want to be there too."

Javier brushed aside Luis's demand. "Only Alonso and Esteban are coming. You be prepared for anything. We don't know in what condition they'll be in."

That was the last thing anyone said as they left the camp, drove for three hours to the pick-up site then waited there for an extra two hours. It was already dark when they heard approaching cars. They'd kept their headlights on and were now standing in the glare, showing the guerrillas they were alone and unarmed.

Then the hostages were coming out of the second Jeep. A man, a woman, two boys, Caridad, then at last—Savannah.

Javier knew nothing more. Nothing but that she was in his arms and there were tears. Hers? His? Both? Everything vanished as she flooded his senses. *Mi amor, mi amor* was a litany as he raised his head and moved slightly away, frantic to check she was OK.

She threw herself back into his arms and clung. "I'm OK, darling."

It was only then he remembered. Caridad. The others.

Caridad was in Alonso's arms. They were both weeping, too. So were the others. Javier let out the pent-up breath he'd been holding since he'd heard Savannah inform him of their kidnapping. "Let's get you out of here!"

As he rushed her back to the Jeep, Savannah turned and waved. Waved? His incredulous gaze panned to her former captors, found them all waving back, especially one young guerrilla.

All right. He'd wake up any moment, suffocating and nowhere nearer rescuing Savannah. What else explained this bizarre farewell?

*   *   *

"Thanks for the happy-release party, guys." Savannah stood up, dragged Javier up with her. "I'll tell you more stories later. Now, if you'll excuse me and Javier…!"

Savannah ran all the way up to their hotel room, unable to wait to get him alone at last. It had been seven hours since they'd been released. Once Javier had made sure they were all OK, he'd insisted they drive back to Neiva where he'd checked them all into the same hotel. Considering her agitation, she'd been grateful he hadn't taken her back home.

Her agitation had nothing to do with surviving her kidnapping, though. She'd stopped fearing the guerrillas after Gomes and Diaz had helped her during Herrera's surgery, then she'd become a favorite after she'd saved two of their own after an almost fatal assault by a rival faction. All her tension and jitters were accounted for by being back with Javier, wanting to ask him what she hadn't the day she'd been kidnapped.

Ask him now! "Javier…" He took her words, her lips, her soul in silence, with burning intensity.

Then he took her, against the door, then on the floor, then on the bed. That last time she took him as fiercely, at last telling him everything. "I love you, Javier, love you. I can't live without you. You're my life—my life, darling…"

Her confessions sent a shudder through him, provoking both shock and his most powerful climax, but no reciprocation. Not even the usual endearments. Her heart shriveled even as her body was caught up in the conflagration, convulsing in transfiguring ecstasy with him, beneath him.

When they lay still merged, still shuddering, it wasn't his beloved weight that suffocated her but his silence. Then he was withdrawing. It felt like the end.

She clung to him. "Javier. Marry me."

She'd laughed when he'd asked her. But now he was wrenching himself out of her arms. That wasn't fair retaliation. Her rejection had hurt his ego, his extinguished her soul.

He got up and started dressing. *Déjà vu.* The night he'd walked out on her was replaying almost frame for frame.

"So now we're even?"

"Even?" He swung around at her hoarse whisper, in his unbuttoned jeans, his formidable body bunched, just as it had been when she'd begged him to come back to bed more than three years ago. *"Even?"*

"It didn't cross your mind? I don't care if it did. I love you, Javier. I know you don't think I'm capable of love, and I don't blame you. I don't have any example of lasting relationships in my family or in my own life. But I love you, I've always loved you. I just didn't know what it was, wasn't ready to handle it or equipped to do it justice. But now I am. I *am*, Javier."

His face clenched in a horrible grimace as if he was about to cry. Then he closed his eyes, exhaled. When he opened them, an artificial almost-smile hovered around their edges. "I've already said marriage would have been a huge mistake, and it still would be. But that doesn't mean we can't be together somehow. Your time in Colombia is over, but we don't have to be, even if we only manage to meet a couple of weeks out of each year."

A couple of weeks? After all they'd been through, she was still only good for temporary sex in his eyes? What would he do for the rest of the year—settle down with someone he didn't consider it a mistake to marry? What would she be? His annual marital vacation? Had she been so wrong about him, about everything? Was that it, her final, fatal miscalculation?

Lying there naked, needy, waiting for him to take pity on her was too much. Dragging herself to her knees, putting on her clothes under his burning gaze, was like nothing she'd ever felt. Not even when she'd thought she'd be murdered, after heaven only knew how much abuse. So this was despair.

"Savannah…"

Her eyes went to his, still hoping, still praying. This intensity. Was he finding it hard to walk away from her this time? Would he change his mind?

No.

His stilted smile made her sick. "What do you say? I'll come to you, every available day."

So he *was* offering her what she'd once offered him. Was he really getting even?

End this. Just get out of here. "Forget it, Javier. Forget everything I said tonight. I must have lost my head after my ordeal. When I leave, as soon as the MSU's mission is over, we won't—"

"You don't have to!"

"Don't have to what?"

"Stay until the mission is over."

Oh.

Did he have to sound so eager to get rid of her? Did he have to wipe out all her delusions of usefulness and purpose, of her value to him? Tonight of all nights, when she'd almost become certain? During their release, she'd felt as if he'd been dying without her, fearing for her. His lovemaking had felt like the breath he'd been suffocating for. But that had only been what she'd wanted to see and feel.

Here was the truth. Cheap, ugly…nightmarish. Would he have cared if her captors had killed her? Had he been more than a convenient local to convey the ransom money and collect her? Had she been more than a convenient body to slake his lust with during the hard, harsh toil? Could she live on if she lost her faith in him?

She was dressed now, covered, lifeless. "I'll call my father. I may as well make use of his presence and private jet."

The jet was already moving, gliding towards the runway. Javier's feet pounded the tarmac harder, outstripping the pursuing airport security by hundreds of meters now. They hadn't already fired at him only because they'd made sure he was unarmed at the gates. They just thought he was suicidal.

And they weren't far from the truth. If he couldn't stop Savannah… No. That wasn't an option.

He was now in the jet's path. The pilot dodged him but Javier just intercepted him once more.

He'd tried to contact Savannah a hundred times, but her cell phone was turned off. When he'd contacted the jet, Jacob Richardson had ordered the pilot to ignore him. But he couldn't let her leave without telling her what he'd been too stunned to say last night, the answer to everything that he'd been unable to see till he'd seen her walking out of his life. He had to do it *now*, even if it was the last thing he ever did.

Which it might be. The jet wasn't stopping.

Suddenly Savannah appeared in the cockpit.

Savannah.

Too much to say, to feel. He just opened his arms, silently begging her to fill them.

The jet stopped. In seconds its door opened and she was framed there, just a couple of meters above him, her heavenly eyes tinged with the same hell he was going through. Could it be true—did she really love him? Every unbelievable thing she'd said last night hadn't been said on the rebound, a re-action to survival? But even if it was and she didn't truly feel like that, he'd take it, would make it real, would make her love him, eventually.

"Savannah…" *Just tell her.* "*Te amo tanto—demasiado mi alma! Eres mi vida, mi todo!*"

The pain in her eyes broke loose in tears that brought his own flowing over his numb cheeks. "You love me, I'm your soul, your life, your everything—for two weeks each year?"

"For every second, as long as I live and beyond."

"You mean you want me to stay?"

"*No!*"

She jerked, a new rush of tears deluging her cheeks as she turned on her heel.

Stop her. Tell her. "Savannah, *I'll* come with you!"

That froze her. She turned to him, her streaming eyes in-credulous. "You can't! You have responsibilities, duties, the MSU, your other projects, your people, your family…"

There was one simple truth to it all. "You come first."

He barely caught her. Her hurtling mass as she jumped out of the jet and into his arms drove him to his knees, in every way.

They remained there, kneeling on the tarmac, locked in total surrender to each other. Then she fought out of his hold, her eyes clearing, everything his imagination had never conjured filling them. Love, devotion, belief, selflessness, determination and desire—like he'd never believed existed. "And you come first with me. But you *can't* leave here. And I don't want to leave either. I want to be here with you, working with you, sharing every unique, magnificent, worthwhile moment with you."

"No, Savannah, I'm not putting you in jeopardy again. Why do you think I couldn't wait for you to leave? There's no way to describe the depth of desperation I felt when you were in danger…"

"I wasn't in any real danger!"

"Only because circumstances helped you and had your captors awed by you and indebted to you. Next time—"

"There won't be a next time!"

"I can't take that chance, *amor*. A chunk of my sanity is gone, there's constant fear for ever constricting my soul. I can't exist this way. I must know you're safe, and I can't exist without you any more. All this time I've been looking for ways for you to be with me here, never realizing that the only way to be with you is to go home with you."

"The only home I have is in your arms, whether it's on the road or in your house here."

"I don't even have that house any more, Savannah."

"What?"

Demonios. Why had he said *that*? Now he had to explain. "I sold it."

"*Why?*"

Only a full explanation would satisfy her now. He gritted his teeth and gave it to her. How he'd found the ransom money, his offer to Mendoza, and how her hostage situation had been resolved.

Her dazed gaze roamed his face. "*You* got me out? *Everyone* gave you *all* their money to get me out?"

She surged into him, racked by sobs that escalated into uncontrollable weeping. "Oh, my love—my love! You offered yourself for me and you think I'll let you sacrifice any more?"

He soothed her. "The only sacrifice is being without you. I'll find a way to continue my work from the US. I don't have to be hands-on to be of use. And with your help, our work will reach even more people. If I need to be here in person, I'll come back, do what needs to be done, then run home to you."

"No, Javier. You won't. Just accept it now and let's get on with our lives."

"Even without the danger, I can't let you live here. I don't even have a home to offer you any more."

"You think it would be a sacrifice for me, living here? Being with you anywhere is my ultimate reward, Javier. Can't you believe that? You still can't believe in me?"

"I believe in nothing like I believe in you."

"Then believe this—I'll never sit in an empty, luxurious, so-called safe house and wait for you. I'll never leave your side again. So let's just continue our work, wherever it takes us, let's live anywhere as long as we're together. I promise I'll be more careful."

Her determination, her conviction! He hadn't thought it possible to fall deeper or love more fully. He'd been wrong.

"Say yes."

What else could he say? "Yes."

A cough had them both looking up. It was Jacob Richardson.

"Have you damaged your knees enough? Maybe you'd like to continue your undying declarations in more comfort up here?"

Javier met the blue eyes of the older, male version of the woman he adored. He no longer saw revulsion and antagonism in them. Or maybe he just wanted to believe that. His feelings towards Savannah's father had changed, too. Gone were the defensiveness and the resentment. A strange empathy replaced those, a bond. They were united in loving Savannah, in wanting to protect her, to provide her with only the best.

Javier swept Savannah up and looked up at Richardson. "I'm asking for your daughter's hand in marriage, Dr. Richardson."

One haughty blond eyebrow rose. "You can ask, and I can say no way."

Savannah tensed in his arms. He gave her a reassuring squeeze.

Her father lowered his eyebrow, exhaled. "Why are you asking me? Savannah has proved she's her own woman, capable of taking on the world better than anyone I know, better than me. I don't have any say in her life any more."

The thrill that went through Savannah at her father's admission surged through Javier, along with happiness for her for getting that much-needed validation. He was beginning to like the man. "No, you don't. Not through orders or manipulation. But you're welcome to have a say in her life through the claims of love. In mine, too, if you want."

Savannah jumped in his arms, kissed him full on the lips. Oh, she approved of his words, did she? He smiled his love and pleasure into her delighted, delightful eyes.

The jet's steps were now in place and Jacob descended to stand facing them. His words were ragged when they finally came. "I'm sorry, Savannah, for everything. I put you in danger, and I made so many mistakes raising you after your mother left us. It doesn't matter that it was out of love, out of fearing for you, wanting the best for you…"

Savannah hurled herself at him, silencing him. "If you love me, it's the only thing that matters. But Javier was also going to let me go because he feared for me and wanted the best for me. Well, *I* know what's best for me. It's to be on best terms with you, Daddy, and to be with Javier, for better or worse!''

Her father hugged her tighter. ''Just as long as you forget this crazy idea of going to the Badovnan frontline!''

Javier's hair all stood on end. *''What?''*

He no longer saw or heard the other man. He swept Savannah towards him, anxiety smothering him once more. ''Forget it, Savannah. You're not going. I was going to pieces having you here, in *possible* danger, I'm damned if I'll let you go where there's *certain* danger!''

She extricated herself from his hands and stood back, hands on hips, her expression unfathomable. ''One dictator repents and another is born, huh? *You're* telling me what to do now?''

''You bet I am! As you get to tell me what to do.''

''I do?''

''Yes. Anything. Tell me to do anything and I'll do it.''

Her eyes gleamed. ''You're only saying that because you think I'll never ask you anything that goes against your wishes.''

She had to be tormenting him for letting her walk out last night, for not falling to his knees the moment she'd asked him to marry him. ''You're really thinking of leaving me and going to the front line?''

''This was before I came here. I told my father that after Colombia I'd go to Badovna.''

''But you no longer want to?'' He still needed to hear her confirmation.

Her tinkling laugh rang out. ''It would be difficult to go there while I'm pregnant.''

He went hot, then cold, then burning. ''You—you mean in the future…?''

''I mean now!''

Savannah watched him change color. She'd stunned him, that was for sure! But what else? What was that volatile emotion blazing from him? ''I—I know I was careless but—''

His hard, compulsive kiss silenced her, and her doubts. "*We* were. And then we were no such thing. We were both telling each other how committed to one another we are, in the most revealing, effective way."

Savannah saw everything in his eyes at that moment. His whole being, their entwined fate, their children, robust and loved. She threw herself into arms strong enough to create the best future for them all. Then she turned and hugged her father, secure that a new chapter in their relationship was about to start, too. Turning to Javier, she whispered. "Take me home, my love."

He opened his arms.

Later that night, they were back in their hotel room. Javier had refused to let Savannah's father buy him back his house, only letting him pay his debts to those who'd lent him the ransom money. Now they were lying entwined in bed, planning their future according to their changing priorities. Not to mention getting each last insecurity and question out of the way.

"I have only one last grievance, *mi vida*."

Savannah's heart contracted. Until he smiled, if a little uncertainly. "Your hair. Why did you cut it?"

The answer was simple. "It was useless when I couldn't wrap it around you."

He buried his face in it now, breathed her in raggedly. "*Ah, mi amor.*"

"*Te amo, Javier. Eres mi todo.* You and our baby." Suddenly her breath hitched. She had one last thing she needed to tell him. "And speaking of our baby... As much as I love your big family…"

"You do? I thought they horrified you!"

"No way. I just wanted to leave because they told me I'd never be with you."

His scowl was spectacular. Her champion. "Who said that? Just tell me and I'll—"

"You'll do nothing. It's between sisters now. But speaking of sisters, and no matter how wonderful it is to have so many, I don't think I'll have more than two babies. Not because I don't want to have as many babies as possible with you, but because I want to be there with you every available moment, working with you. More babies would—"

He came over her again, stopped her words in his mouth. "Two are more than enough. One is, *mi amor*."

He entered her slowly, groaned his pleasure as he slid inside her, his tender eyes echoing everything in the heart that surrounded him even before her body did, dissipating the last of her apprehension. "Even if there hadn't been any babies, you would have been enough for me. You *are*. More than I ever hoped for. *Believe* that."

She finally did. And as he took her to their own dimension of ecstasy, she clung to him and whispered, "I believe you, my love. In you and in me. In us."

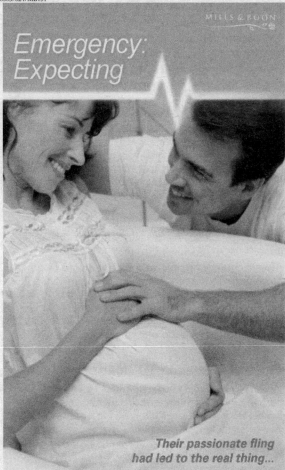

MILLS & BOON

Emergency:
Expecting

**Their passionate fling
had led to the real thing...**

Carol Marinelli Sarah Morgan Lilian Darcy

On sale 6th May 2005

*Available at most branches of WHSmith, Tesco, ASDA, Martins,
Borders, Eason, Sainsbury's and all good paperback bookshops.*

MILLS & BOON®

Live the emotion

Playboy Lovers

They're the most eligible bachelors around
– but can they fall in love?

In June 2005, By Request brings back
three favourite romances by our
bestselling Mills & Boon authors

The Secretary's Seduction *by Jane Porter*
The Prospective Wife *by Kim Lawrence*
The Playboy Doctor *by Sarah Morgan*

Make sure you get hold of these
passionate stories,
on sale 3rd June 2005

FREE

4 BOOKS AND A SURPRISE GIFT!

We would like to take this opportunity to thank you for reading this Mills & Boon® book by offering you the chance to take FOUR more specially selected titles from the Medical Romance™ series absolutely FREE! We're also making this offer to introduce you to the benefits of the Reader Service™—

- ★ **FREE home delivery**
- ★ **FREE gifts and competitions**
- ★ **FREE monthly Newsletter**
- ★ **Books available before they're in the shops**
- ★ **Exclusive Reader Service offers**

Accepting these FREE books and gift places you under no obligation to buy; you may cancel at any time, even after receiving your free shipment. Simply complete your details below and return the entire page to the address below. You don't even need a stamp!

YES! Please send me 4 free Medical Romance books and a surprise gift. I understand that unless you hear from me, I will receive 6 superb new titles every month for just £2.75 each, postage and packing free. I am under no obligation to purchase any books and may cancel my subscription at any time. The free books and gift will be mine to keep in any case.

M5ZEE

Ms/Mrs/Miss/Mr......................................Initials ....
BLOCK CAPITALS PLEASE

Surname ....

Address ....

....

....Postcode ....

Send this whole page to:
The Reader Service, FREEPOST CN81, Croydon, CR9 3WZ

Offer valid in UK only and is not available to current Reader Service™ subscribers to this series. Overseas and Eire please write for details. We reserve the right to refuse an application and applicants must be aged 18 years or over. Only one application per household. Terms and prices subject to change without notice. Offer expires 31st August 2005. As a result of this application, you may receive offers from Harlequin Mills & Boon and other carefully selected companies. If you would prefer not to share in this opportunity please write to The Data Manager at PO Box 676, Richmond, TW9 1WU.

Mills & Boon® is a registered trademark owned by Harlequin Mills & Boon Limited.
Medical Romance™ is being used as a trademark. The Reader Service™ is being used as a trademark.